THE FILL-IN BOYFRIEND

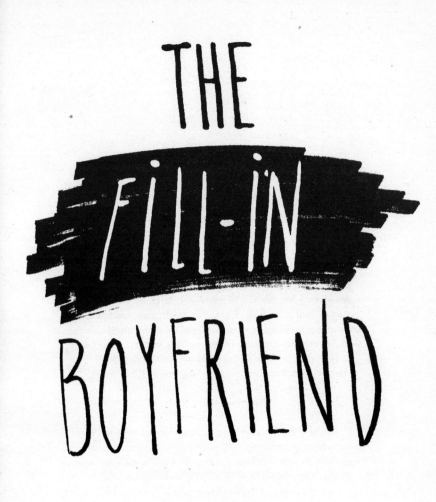

THE FILL-IN BOYFRIEND

KASIE WEST

SCHOLASTIC INC.

To Dad, who taught me to read for knowledge,
and to Mom, who taught me to read for fun.
Love you both.

ISBN 978-0-545-90306-6

12 11 10 9 8 7 6 5 4   16 17 18 19 20/0

Printed in the U.S.A.   40

First Scholastic printing, September 2015

Typography by Torborg Davern

CHAPTER 1

In some part of my brain, probably the logical part that seemed to be missing at the moment, I knew I should let go and walk away, maintain some of my dignity. Instead, I gripped his waist more securely by wrapping my arms around him and pressed my cheek against his chest. Logic was definitely not ruling my brain right now. Desperation was. And even though I knew desperation wasn't attractive, I couldn't help myself.

He sighed, releasing some air, which allowed me to tighten my hold even more. *Isn't that how boa constrictors kill their prey?* Not even this thought made me let go.

1

"Gia, I'm sorry."

"Then don't do this. And if you have to, can't it wait two hours?"

"The fact that you said that makes me know it can't. You only care about your friends seeing me."

"That's not true." Okay, so it was kinda true. But only because of Jules. She'd infiltrated our group a year ago and ever so slowly tried to turn my best friends against me. Her latest claim was that I'd been lying about having a boyfriend for the last two months. So yes, I wanted my friends to see that I had not been lying. That it was she who was trying to divide our group in half. She who was at least one quarter evil. Not me.

That wasn't the only reason I'd wanted Bradley to come tonight. I had really liked him before he decided to break up with me in the parking lot at prom. But now that he'd pulled out the jerk card, I just needed him to walk inside, prove that he existed, maybe punch Jules in the gut for me, and then walk out. Was that too much to ask? Plus, hello, this was my senior prom. He was *really* going to make me walk alone into my senior prom, where I would possibly be crowned royalty tonight?

"That's not all I care about. . . ." My voice cracked even though I was trying not to show weakness. Well, aside from the whole clinging-to-him-like-a-static-filled-sock thing.

"It's all you care about and you confirmed it tonight when you saw me and the first thing you said was 'My friends are going to die.' Really, Gia? That's the first thing you say when you see me after two weeks?"

My mind raced back. Was that really what I had said or was he making things up now to try to make himself feel better? He did look really good. And yes, I did want my friends to see just how good he looked. Could he blame me for that?

"And the whole way over here you were trying to plan how we were going to walk in. You told me exactly how to look at you."

"So I'm slightly controlling. You knew that about me."

"Slightly?"

A car pulled into the empty space across from where I was squeezing the life out of my boyfriend . . . my ex-boyfriend. A couple climbed out of the backseat. I didn't recognize either of them.

"Gia." Bradley pried my hands apart and stepped back. "I have to go. It's a long drive home."

He did at least look sincerely sorry.

I crossed my arms, finally finding a little dignity far too late. "Fine. Go."

"You should go inside anyway. You look amazing."

"Can you just cuss me out and walk away or something?

I don't need to think you're sweet after all this." He *was* sweet and the thought that my desperation to keep him here was about more than just my friends was battling to take over my emotions. I pushed it back. I did not want him to know he'd really hurt me.

He smiled his playful smile then raised his voice. "I never want to talk to you again. You're a shallow, self-centered snob and you deserve to walk in there alone!"

Why did that sound so convincing? I kept up our little charade. "I hate you, jerk!"

He blew me a kiss and I smiled. I watched him until he got in the car and left. My smile slipped off my face as my stomach tightened. Guess he was assuming I'd find a ride home. Thank goodness all my friends were inside . . . waiting for me to show up with the guy I'd bragged about for the last two months. I growled, trying to turn my hurt into anger, and leaned up against the tailgate of a red truck. That's when I caught the eye of a guy sitting in the driver's seat of the car across from me. I quickly straightened up from my slumped position— not even a stranger got to see me looking weak—and he dropped his gaze.

What was some guy doing sitting in his car? He lifted a book and began to read. He was reading? Sitting in the parking lot at prom and reading? Then it hit me: the couple that had climbed out of the backseat. He was dropping someone off. A younger sister or brother, maybe.

I assessed him while he read. I couldn't see much but he wasn't bad to look at. Brown hair, olive skin. He could've even been tall—his head was higher than the headrest—but it was hard to tell. He wasn't my type at all—hair a little too shaggy, on the thin side, glasses— but he'd have to do. I walked to his window. He was reading some geography book or something about the world in eighty days. I tapped on his window and he slowly looked up. It took him even longer to roll down the window.

"Hi," I said.

"Hey."

"Do you go here?" If he went to school here and I just hadn't met him before, this wouldn't work. Because odds were people would know him.

"What?"

"Do you go to school here?"

"No. We just moved here, but I'm finishing out the year at my old school."

Even better. They were new to the area. "You're here dropping off your brother?"

"Sister."

"Perfect."

He raised his eyebrows.

"You get to be my date."

"Uh . . ." His mouth opened but that's all that came out.

"Do you live close? Because you can't go in there in jeans and a T-shirt. Especially one with a telephone booth on it."

His eyes flickered to his shirt and then back to me. "A telephone booth? Seriously?"

"Do you at least have some dark pants and a button-down shirt? Maybe a tie? A teal tie would be awesome to match me but I'm not holding my breath about that." I tilted my head. He really didn't look like my type. My friends would know this. "And do you happen to own contacts and some hair product?"

"I'm just going to roll up my window now."

"No. Please." I put my hand on top. Had I ever had a night where I felt so desperate? "My boyfriend just broke up with me. I'm sure you saw. And I really don't want to walk into my senior prom alone. Plus my friends didn't think he existed. Long story, but I need you to be him. Two hours. That's all I'm asking for. Besides, you're just sitting here anyway waiting for your sister." Crap. His sister. Was she going to yell his name across the gym and ruin this for me? We'd just have to avoid her. Or let her in on the secret. I hadn't decided yet. "It will be way more fun than sitting in a parking lot."

He was still looking at me like I was crazy. I felt crazy. "You want me to pretend to be Captain America?" He pointed toward the street.

I was confused at first but then realized that's what he was calling Bradley, whose build was on the beefy side. "They've never met him, so they have no idea what he looks like. Besides you're . . ." I gestured toward him without finishing the sentence. I tried to think of a different superhero to compare him to but nothing came to mind. I wasn't well versed in superheroes. Were there some who were on the thinner side? Spiderman? That didn't seem like a compliment.

He just sat there, staring at me, waiting for me to finish the sentence.

"I can pay you."

He raised his eyebrows. "I'm sure there are services for that. Maybe you can try calling 1-800-HOOKERS or something?"

I rolled my eyes but couldn't help the smile that came with it. "You know that number well?"

He let out a single laugh.

"Fine. If you feel weird about taking money, I'll owe you."

"Owe me what?"

"I don't know. . . . If you're ever in need of a fake date, I'll be there for you."

"I'm not exactly in the habit of requiring fake dates."

"Well, fine. I'm glad you can get a real date whenever you want, but I can't. Well, I mean, I usually can, but obviously not right now in the middle of an empty parking lot." Was I going to have to pull out some fake tears to get me a fake date?

"Fine."

"Fine?" I was surprised even though I'd really hoped he'd say yes.

"Yes. I live six blocks from here. I'll go change into something more prom worthy." He rolled up the window while muttering something about how he didn't believe he was going along with this. Then he drove away.

I stood there for five minutes wondering if that was just his way of getting out of this whole thing. He probably texted his sister and told her just to call when she needed a ride home. And if he only lived six blocks away, why was he waiting in the parking lot anyway? Shouldn't he have driven home and waited there?

I pulled out my phone and checked Instagram and Twitter to make sure Bradley hadn't said anything about our breakup. There was nothing. It didn't surprise me; Bradley wasn't online that much. Another reason Jules thought I'd made him up. I sent off a tweet about how prom was going to rock and then tucked my phone back into my clutch that matched my dress perfectly.

Another ten minutes passed and I was sure he wasn't coming back now. I started thinking of all the excuses I was going to give my friends when I got inside. He got sick. He had to study for finals for his college classes on Monday . . . because he's in college.

I sighed. This was pathetic. The truth. I needed to tell the truth. He broke up with me in the parking lot. My eyes stung with tears over that thought. Bradley broke up with me in a parking lot. I'd screwed up and lost him and now I might lose more than just him. Would this be the final piece of evidence my friends needed to believe the claims Jules had made? I knew the look I'd get from Jules right away when I told the truth. It would be the yeah-right-he-doesn't-exist look. The look she gave me every time I mentioned Bradley. It was the look that always made me tell more stories. Too bad I'd told so many that even my other friends had started to question his existence.

We'd met in a café at UCLA when we were there for a film festival my older brother was involved with. Alone in the café, Bradley had thought I was a student there. I didn't correct him because I was actually going to be a student there next year. I'd just gotten my early acceptance that very weekend so I had been feeling quite collegiate. We'd exchanged phone numbers and texted for a while. And what started off as mere attraction became more. He told stupid jokes and knew so much about so many places from all his traveling. He was interesting. A couple of weeks later, I came clean about my age. By that time, we liked each other. The main problem was that I lived three hours from UCLA. So he'd only come up a couple of times in the two months we'd been dating and hadn't met my friends. And now, it was over.

I threw back my shoulders and faced the gym doors. I didn't need a date, real or otherwise. My friends liked me regardless of who I was or wasn't with. Even as I thought it, I wished for it to be true. I couldn't lose my boyfriend and my friends all in one night. I needed them in my life. As I started to walk, headlights cast my shadow on the asphalt in front of me. I turned as the car and lights went off.

The guy stepped out. "Were you going to go in there without me after all that begging?"

CHAPTER 2

• • • • • • •

I smiled. I couldn't help it. He was actually wearing a suit—black, with a light gray tie. His glasses were gone and he was tall.

This was exactly what I needed. We'd be seen. He could break up with me at the end of the night. No smug looks from Jules, no pity sighs from Laney, and no just-tell-the-truth head tilts from Claire. And it would be close to the truth. My fill-in guy was just rearranging tonight's order of events for me a little. There was no harm in that. Especially if it kept the quarter-evil Jules at bay.

"Hi," I said, approaching his car, where he still stood by the open door as if he hadn't completely committed to this idea yet. "You look great." My eyes went to his hair that I could see better now that I was closer. It was a mess. A mess that he had tried to tame, it seemed.

"Sit for a sec." I pointed to the seat of his car. He raised an eyebrow but obeyed. I fished out a small comb from my clutch and used it to style his hair. When it was off his forehead and shaped nicely I gave a satisfied nod. "You clean up well."

He let out a sigh. "Let's get this over with."

He stood and offered me an elbow. I grabbed his hand instead and pulled him toward the gym.

"Whoa. Hold on there," he said, my body jerking to a halt, which wasn't very fun in my heels. "I need a little backstory here. You are trying to convince your friends we actually know each other, yes?"

"Oh, right. Let's see."

"A name would be a good start."

I laughed. I hadn't even told him my name. "I'm Gia Montgomery. Seventeen. Senior here at lovely Freemont High. I'm on the student council and don't usually have to beg for dates. As in, I never have before today."

"Noted."

"And for the next two hours you are Bradley Harris.

Junior at UCLA, which is why my parents disapprove, by the way. They think you're way too old for me."

"I am," he said.

I wasn't sure if he was talking about Bradley or himself. I thought he had implied earlier that he was in high school. "How old are you?"

"If I'm a junior that would make me at least, what? Twenty-one?"

He was talking about Bradley. I rolled my eyes. "Yes. But that's only four years older than me."

"Which wouldn't be the end of the world if you weren't still in high school. And underage."

"I'm only in high school for five more weeks and you sound like my parents now."

He shrugged. "They sound like good parents."

"Well, it doesn't matter anymore. At the end of the night you get to break up with me. In front of my friends, preferably. Try not to make a big show of it. Quickly and quietly. Then, like the real Bradley, you can walk away forever and this will be over." A lump formed in my throat as I said that, as I pictured Bradley walking away from me as if it was the easiest thing in the world to do. I pushed the image away and offered him a smile.

"I can handle that."

"Good. So what about your sister? Is she going to give us trouble in there? Run across the gym screaming your name?"

"No. My sister will not expect me to be in there, looking like this. And she's really into her date. But if I see her coming, I'll make sure to head her off and fill her in. She's cool. She'll play along."

"Why don't you text her? Just in case."

"I would, but in my quick change, I forgot my phone." He patted his pockets to show me he was serious.

"She'll be cool?"

"She'll be cool."

"Okay, I think we're set, then."

He smirked at me like I was missing something obvious.

"What?"

"Nothing. Let's go." He had a slow, confident step as he walked with me to the gym. He didn't even seem to mind holding my hand.

Just inside the door I handed over to the teacher behind the table the tickets I had purchased for Bradley and me and we continued into the main room. The music was loud—a live band—and not very good. The band was the winner of the auditions we had held for this event, so they were the best of the worst. Last year we had hired a popular local band, but with "more affordable" ticket prices, Mr. Lund said we didn't have the budget for it this year.

I saw my friends and their dates across the room, standing around a high table. I closed my eyes for a moment and channeled every ounce of acting ability I had in my body, which wasn't very much but would have to do. Beside me, my fill-in date didn't even seem nervous. Of course he wasn't—he had nothing to lose.

"My sister is dancing, so I think we're good for now," he said.

I followed his gaze to a girl dressed in blue—the skirt of the dress full of puffy layers. She was cute—long brown hair, friendly face. I'd never seen her before in my life so she must've been younger than me. Although he had said they just moved here, so maybe they'd moved here very recently. I didn't recognize her date either, though, so I went back to the younger theory.

"Okay. So, will you try to look at me like you're madly in love?"

"Captain America and you were madly in love?"

I opened my mouth—my first instinct was to say "of course"—but stopped myself because it wasn't true. Bradley and I were . . . Well, we were happy. At least I'd thought we were before tonight. I put on my best teasing smile, glad that my feelings, which had tried to take over in the parking lot, were back in my control. "Do you not have a reference point for that emotion?"

He concentrated for a moment then turned a smoldering gaze on me. Wow. He was good.

"That may be a little thick."

He softened the intensity of his gaze and for the first time I noticed his eyes were blue. Not good. Bradley had brown eyes.

"That bad, huh?"

"No. Your look is great." Meaning he did know what being in love felt like. I was the one without a reference point. "Your eye color is frustrating."

"I've never been told that before. Thanks."

"I'm sorry. I'm sure girls tell you that they're dreamy or whatever." And they were. "It's just . . ."

"Bradley has emerald green? No, melty chocolate brown?"

I laughed because he had grabbed his chest and said it in a melodramatic voice. "Yes. Very melty."

He met my eyes. "Like yours."

"Well, his are more chocolate, mine are more sepia, but . . ." I shook my head, trying to get back on subject. "Just try not to make eye contact with anyone."

"Because that won't be creepy. You think your friends remember the eye color of a guy they've never met? Did you really talk about his eyes that much?"

"No. I mean, well, they've seen a few pictures."

"They've seen pictures?" His eyes widened. "And you think we're going to get away with this how?"

"Well, they were from a distance. And one was of half his face." Much to my frustration, he wasn't a fan of having his picture taken. "It's been a while since they've seen them. I think you look similar enough that it will work. But work on the non-creepy version of the no-eye-contact thing."

He took my hand in his, kissed it, gave me his smoldering stare, and said, "Well, I only have eyes for you anyway."

He was *really* good. I laughed. "I see my friends. Let's go."

"Why didn't your friends think I existed if they've seen pics?" he asked as we made our way through dancing bodies.

"Because you went to UCLA and I was usually the one visiting you. When you did come up here, you wanted to spend our time together, not with my friends."

"So I'm a snob. Got it."

"I didn't say that."

"When you came to visit me, did we hang out with my friends?"

"No. We rarely saw each other. We didn't want to have to deal with other people when we did."

"Okay, so you were my secret."

"No, it's how I wanted it too. And besides, you just drove three hours to come to my prom, so you were obviously planning on meeting all my friends." It was weirding me out that we were talking like he really was Bradley. I shook my head. "*He* was planning to meet my friends."

"And yet *he* broke up with you in the parking lot before he actually did."

I bit the inside of my cheek. Ten more steps and we'd reach the group, so I couldn't explain to him that I had treated Bradley poorly. That the first thing I'd said to him after not having seen him for two weeks was that my friends were going to die. It was because he'd looked so amazing. But I should've said that instead. I shouldn't have worried what my friends were going to think. It was hard not to, though, when I'd spent two months fielding questions about his existence, two months telling them all about him. All because of Jules. I shouldn't have let her get to me like I did.

Claire noticed me first and her eyes seemed to light up in relief when she saw my date. We were the closest, so she was always the one defending me. "Gia!" At her exclamation everyone else turned around.

The look from Jules was priceless. It was a smug smile followed by a slight drop of her jaw. And for once, Laney didn't have the pity face. I smiled a huge smile.

"Everyone, this is Bradley."

He raised his hand in a small wave and I didn't know if it was to be funny or if it was unintentional, but when he said "Nice to meet you all," his voice was low and husky.

Claire widened her eyes at me like way-to-go-Gia was written in them.

Jules got her inner snob back quickly as she looked him up and down. I held my breath, waiting for her to say he looked nothing like his pictures or nothing like the guys I normally dated. Instead she said, "I'm surprised you wanted to come to a high school prom."

He looked me straight in the eyes and slipped his arm down my back, hooking me around the waist. "It was important to Gia." With the words he pulled me against his side. My back tingled with his touch. My first instinct was to yank away, but that wouldn't have been my reaction to Bradley. I would've leaned into him. I would've sighed happily. I made myself do both.

Jules smirked. "Is that the theme of your relationship? 'The importance of Gia'?" She actually did air quotes.

Garrett, Jules's date, laughed but then stopped quickly when another one of the guys smacked him on the back.

"No," my date said before I had a chance to respond. "But maybe it should be."

With this, they all laughed. I was too busy glaring at Jules to laugh.

"We're going to dance," my date said. And as he led me to the dance floor, it hit me that I didn't know his real name. Was that what the smirk was all about when we were walking toward the gym? So when the-guy-whose-name-I-didn't-know put his arms around me, I leaned my forehead against his chest and whispered, "Sorry."

CHAPTER 3

• • • • • • •

"What are you sorry for?" fill-in Bradley asked.

"I don't even know your real name."

He laughed a low chuckle that I could feel through his chest. Then he leaned down so his breath tickled my ear when he said, "My name is Bradley."

I looked up with a gasp. "Really?"

He shook his head no. "I'm a method actor. I have to become a person."

"Are you an actor?" It wouldn't have surprised me. He was obviously really good at it.

He looked up, thinking. "You didn't tell me that about myself. Am I?"

I hit his chest with a laugh. "Stop."

He glanced over my shoulder, toward where my friends were still standing. "Nice friends you got there."

"They're mostly nice. Jules is just constantly trying to oust me."

"Why?"

"I have no idea. I think she thinks I'm the alpha of our pack and that there is only room for one without resorting to cannibalism."

"I'm going to take your weird wolf analogy and assume you mean that she wants to be the leader of your group."

I shrugged and watched across the room as Jules hooked her arm through Claire's and said something to her. "It's the only thing I can think of. She's the main reason I needed you here tonight. She thinks I've been lying. I didn't want to give her ammo. She already finds enough without me handing her some on a silver platter."

He raised his eyebrows—he liked to do that, I was already learning. "So if she finds out you've been lying . . . ?"

"Yes. I get it. That's exactly what I'm now doing and wasn't doing before. But she thinks I was. And if I walked in here without you, I would've been gone."

"You don't trust that your other friends like you enough not to let her do that?"

"They like me. But for two months she's been working on this. She really thought she had something on me. She thought I was hiding something. I needed tonight."

"So if you really are the alpha, why aren't you the one kicking her out?"

I'd thought about that question a lot. The main answer was that I really didn't think I was in charge, as much as Jules thought I was. But the other answer, the one I admitted only on my darkest nights, was that I was worried if I made everyone pick, they'd choose her. I was worried that no matter how much confidence I'd shown on the outside, deep down people didn't like me. And that maybe they were right not to. I was not going to tell him that, though. He'd already seen enough weakness tonight. "Because I'm only an eighth evil."

"What?"

"I sometimes call Jules a quarter evil. But that's the thing. . . . I guess I don't want to be that girl. The one who needs to kick someone out of a group. I've been hoping we can work it out, sign a peace treaty, find neutral ground, I don't know." And regardless of the other reasons I was scared to cause trouble, these reasons were true too. I just wanted us all to get along.

"You like analogies, don't you?"

"Yes, I do. Words are powerful."

He tilted his head as if intrigued by that answer. "So, I still don't get it. If they've seen pictures of him, why don't they believe he existed?"

I gave a humorless laugh. "Because there aren't enough of them. But it's not like we were together a lot to take pictures. We have . . . had . . . a long-distance relationship. So Jules thinks I asked some random guy off the street to pose with me."

He laughed. "I don't know why she'd ever think that."

My cheeks flushed red and I looked at the ground. "Yeah. Yeah." It was pretty pathetic that I had to bring in a fake date tonight. A date I wouldn't have had to bring in if my very real boyfriend hadn't broken up with me.

"Are you okay? Upset about the whole Captain America thing?"

I took a breath in through my nose, making sure my voice didn't sound wobbly when I said, "Nope. I'll be fine. We obviously weren't that serious. It was a short, long-distance relationship. Nothing big." I wasn't sure if I was trying to convince him or me with that speech.

He was quiet for so long that I looked up to see if he was still listening. His eyes were on me, searching for something I wasn't sure I possessed. The song ended and a fast one took its place. I took a quick step back. "So. Your real name is?"

"We can't afford any slipups tonight, right? As far as you know, my real name is Bradley." Finally he looked away and I could breathe again. He extended his hand to me and when I took it, he spun me around once then pulled me back into his arms, swaying with the beat.

"You're not half bad at this," I said.

"At what? The acting or the dancing?"

"Well, both, but I was talking about the dancing."

"It's because you're the fifth girl who's asked me to fill in for her date at prom. It's forced me to brush up on my dancing skills."

"Whatever."

"So, Gia Montgomery."

"Yes, nameless boy?"

He gave a breathy laugh. "I don't believe you offered me money for this. Do you go around offering people money for random services often?"

"No, usually my smile gets me what I want." I had actually been a little surprised he was so hard to talk out of that car.

"What kinds of things has it gotten you so far?"

"Besides you in a suit?"

He looked down at his clothes as if my mention of the suit reminded him he was wearing it. "This wasn't because of your smile."

"Then why?" I was very curious. He had gone from

trying to roll up his window to agreeing to be my date in a single breath, it seemed.

"Gia!" I turned toward my name and a girl with long blond hair waved at me. "I voted for you!" She pointed up toward the stage where a sparkly tiara sat on a stool, waiting for its wearer. I smiled at her and mouthed thank you. When I looked back at my date, his eyes sparkled with amusement.

"What?"

"I didn't realize I was dancing with royalty."

"No one has been crowned yet, so that statement is completely premature."

"Who was that?" He gestured back toward the blond girl.

"She's in my history class."

He took my arm in his and said, "Guess we better get back to your friends."

The others had moved to an open table with chairs and were sitting around talking about leaving early and doing something more exciting. It was the "more exciting" part they were all trying to agree on. I glanced back up at the stage, knowing I couldn't leave until the royalty was announced. Jules didn't care about that, though. That's probably why she wanted to leave early. She was bitter she hadn't gotten nominated. It wasn't something she admitted out loud—that would be too obvious—but

I saw her lip curl every time someone brought it up.

Laney whispered, "Sorry," when I reached her side. I wasn't sure what she was sorry about . . . maybe the months of not believing me about Bradley? I slid around the back side of the table, still holding tightly to my date's hand, and we sat down facing the dance floor.

Jules stood and held up her phone. "Everyone get closer together, I want to take a picture." We did, and when she got to three, I felt my fake date move behind me a little more, probably using my head to block his face. Jules studied the picture but didn't ask for a retake. Then she turned her attention to fill-in Bradley. "So, what do college guys do for fun? Aside from pick up high school girls, that is."

He didn't flinch at all from the comment. Probably because it didn't really apply to him. "Well, Gia and I are going to a party after this, but it's invite only so that's not very helpful, I guess. Is there an arcade or something you could all go to?" He said this all in the nicest tone so it almost seemed like he was trying to be polite. But he squeezed my knee under the table and I had to bite my lip to keep from laughing. I could've hugged him for saying that to her. "I don't live around here, so I'm not sure what there is to do."

I swear Jules was like a bloodhound, her senses perking up at the first drop of blood. She should be a detective when she grows up because she picks up on the slightest inconsistency of any story. "But if you don't live around here, how did you get invited to a party here?"

Fill-in Bradley was just as quick with his response. "Who said the party was around here?" Then it was like a battle of wills because they both stared at each other. Jules looked away first and I took a small sip of air in relief. I just needed to get through tonight. If she was already sniffing around for trouble, she was bound to figure out that the guy sitting next to me wasn't who I claimed he was.

My date must've seen the worry on my face because he leaned in close with that I'm-in-love look I'd told him to give me and brushed his lips softly against my cheek. My throat tightened. He was a really good actor.

"Don't look so worried," he whispered. "You'll give us away." He tucked a piece of hair behind my ear. "Now giggle like I said something funny."

I did. It wasn't hard to do, but that's when I saw something on the dance floor that stopped my giddy laugh in my throat. His sister. Staring straight at us.

CHAPTER 4

Her eyes squinted in confusion and then she said something to the guy standing next to her. He looked as well then nodded his agreement. With that, they both headed our way.

"Incoming," I whispered.

Fill-in Bradley's gaze followed mine and he smiled like it was no big deal. "I'll take care of this." He stood. I wondered if I should follow him or just sit here and watch. I went with the sit-here-and-watch option.

When he reached his sister she spoke first, pointing at his clothes. He said something back. Then her head whipped to me, a look of anger there. So much for being cool about this.

"What's going on?" Jules hissed. Of course she was the first one to notice. This was all about to blow up in my face. I knew it. I probably deserved it too. I'd done something stupid and it hadn't lasted for more than an hour. I should've just come clean right away: Bradley broke up with me. Claire and Laney would've understood. They would've believed me. They probably would've even taken me to drown my sorrows in ice cream like we did with Claire when she got dumped last year. But I was being insecure.

I stood, looked at Jules, and said, "Something I'm sure you're going to be very happy about." I didn't wait to see her reaction. I just walked to where he was trying to direct his sister away.

"Come on, let's talk about it out here," I heard him say as I approached.

When I reached them she turned on me, her hands on her hips. Something about that look seemed vaguely familiar.

"No," she said. "You do not get to use my brother like this. He's a nice guy and has been hurt by way too many self-serving girls like you in the past."

"Let's not exaggerate, Bec. It was just the one."

"I'm sorry," I said, responding to his sister but looking

at him. "I didn't mean to turn this into a big deal." I faced her. "You're right. I shouldn't have used your brother like this. He is a nice guy."

She nodded once as though surprised I agreed with her so fast. "Yes he is and he doesn't need to deal with someone like you."

"Don't generalize, Bec. You don't even know Gia."

Bec laughed at this. "Is that what she told you? That she doesn't know me? Classic."

"*Do* I know you?" I asked, confused, studying her face again.

"No. You don't," Bec said, but I got the feeling she meant the exact opposite. I tried to remember meeting her at school. Had I been rude? I met a lot of people because I was in leadership, but it was a big school, at least two thousand students. Still, I needed to try harder to remember names and faces.

I pointed back toward the table. "I'm sorry. I'm messing up a lot tonight, but I'm going to take care of this right now. I'll tell them what really happened." This was the moment of truth. I faced my friends, who by this time were all staring at us from across the room. They would either forgive me or they wouldn't. I took a step forward but was jerked to a halt by someone grabbing my hand.

"No. Don't do this. You were right. Jules is at *least* a

quarter evil. She will crucify you."

"It's okay. It'll all work out. My other friends will stick up for me. Thank you so much for your help tonight. You were such a good sport." I stood on my tiptoes and kissed his cheek then whirled around before I changed my mind.

I went through everything I was going to say when I reached the table. I knew Jules would debate me on each and every truth I spoke, so I braced myself for that as well. I'd been deflecting her jabs for months now. I could handle this. I focused on Claire, her concern showing in her expression. I took comfort in that as I reached the table.

"Is everything okay?" Claire asked.

"No, I have to tell you something. Both of you," I said, looking at Laney then back to Claire.

At that moment, fill-in Bradley rushed to my side. "Please, Gia, she means nothing to me."

My mouth dropped open in shock.

"I know what this must look like, but please give me a chance to explain."

If I'd known his real name right then, I would have said it loudly, in a scolding manner, but I didn't. This wasn't exactly the low-key breakup I had been hoping for. He had not only turned my boyfriend into a cheater but was breaking up with me in front of half the school.

I felt my cheeks heat with embarrassment. "No, don't do this. I'll be fine."

"Oh, really? You'll be fine without me? Is that how you feel? You just want me to walk away like you never existed. Well, what about me, Gia? What am I supposed to do without you?" His voice had gotten progressively louder and by the end of his rant he was practically yelling. A lot of people had turned toward the commotion. I had to turn my back on my friends because I felt nervous laughter bubbling up in my throat and I was pretty sure that wasn't the right reaction to this. Anyone else and that speech would've seemed over the top and fake. But he made it work. He sounded desperate. Probably a lot like I'd sounded earlier with Bradley.

I put my hand on his chest and said in a quiet voice, "Don't do this."

His stare was so intense that I forgot for a moment this was all pretend. "I can see your mind is made up. Call me if you'll hear me out." He lowered his head in defeat and then sulked off like I had really broken his heart. If he wasn't in drama, he definitely should've been. I watched as his sister left the gym after him, glaring at me. She probably wasn't trying to back up his story, but her actions only solidified everything he'd just claimed. I stood there, breathing heavily for several heartbeats, trying to will my hot face to change back to its normal temperature, when a pair of arms wrapped around me.

The familiar scent of Claire's perfume assaulted my senses, bringing me out of my shocked haze.

"I'm so sorry," she said. "What a jerk. Was he messing around with that other girl?"

"No. He's not a jerk." And I didn't even know his name.

"Don't defend him, Gia. And don't you dare take him back. You deserve better." I nodded absentmindedly, having the strangest urge to go rushing after him. Instead, I turned on a watery smile and faced my friends. Why was I reacting like this? I didn't even know him. So why did it feel like I'd been broken up with twice tonight?

I shook my head. I had my friends and that was what mattered right now. I wrapped my arms around Claire and glanced at Jules. Surprisingly, she wasn't looking at me. Her stare was focused on the door that fill-in Bradley had just exited through. There was that familiar calculating look on her face, and I wondered what was going through her mind. I was sure of one thing—it wasn't good.

CHAPTER 5

● ● ● ● ● ● ●

My parents were waiting up for me, per usual, when Claire and her date dropped me off. They'd tried to get me to go out with them after prom but I wasn't feeling up to it. They thought it was because I hadn't won prom queen. Maybe that was part of it. Or the fact that Jules had turned from grumpy to happy with the announcement. That could've affected my mood because I did not want to feel this way over a stupid boy.

My mom stretched up from her spot on the couch to look behind me. It took me a moment to realize she was looking for Bradley.

"He's not here," I mumbled.

My dad stood and yawned. I'd made it home. He could go to bed now. "He could've at least walked you up," he said as he gave me a hug and kissed the top of my head.

I really didn't feel like rehashing the night even though I knew my parents would've been happy if I told them that Bradley and I were finished. "I'm tired. Thanks for waiting up." I hugged my mom and then disappeared into my bedroom. I unzipped my prom dress and let it puddle on the floor, not caring enough to hang it carefully. It wasn't really a memory I'd be looking forward to reliving.

I changed into my pajamas then padded to the bathroom to perform my other nighttime rituals of washing my face and brushing my teeth. When I went back to my room and saw my dress, blue eyes flashed through my mind. I was surprised that was the memory my mind decided to give me with the dress. Why had he agreed to be my fake date anyway? He said it wasn't my smile but we'd been interrupted before he'd answered what it really was. Curiosity burned in my chest. Maybe he thought I was cute? I did look great in that dress.

I gently picked it up and placed it over my desk chair. Why was I analyzing his motives anyway? It didn't matter. My brain was tired. I needed sleep.

But my brain wouldn't shut off. It kept analyzing. It thought about prom and how half the school had witnessed fake Bradley's breakup performance. They'd all be talking about it tomorrow. I didn't need anyone feeling sorry for me. How could I smooth that over? I pulled up Twitter.

Guess I'm single again. Who's throwing me a party?

There. Now everyone would know I was perfectly fine. Because I was. Perfectly fine. I stared at the screen, an urge to delete that tweet rising up my chest. Sleep. I just needed sleep. Everything would be clear in the morning.

Except it wasn't. My mind had chosen to fill the night with dreams of a nameless boy and his mysterious motives. A boy who, even if I wanted to talk to again, was only reachable through a girl who hated my guts. She'd never help me get in touch with her brother. He probably didn't want to talk to me anyway even if the only reason I wanted to talk to him was to satisfy my curiosity.

I wandered downstairs to see my dad at the kitchen table with his sketchpad. I knew better than to disrupt him while he was revisiting a left-behind dream. He had once wanted to be an animator for Disney. Apparently that's a nearly impossible goal. A dream not even close to where he had ended up as a CPA, sitting at a desk, only using the left side of his brain. His pencil glided over the paper with an ease he displayed in no other aspect of his life. He was really good.

The bowls were in the cupboard behind his chair so I opted for a banana and started to take it to my room when he stopped me with a "Good morning, Gia."

"Hey, Dad. Mom at the grocery store?"

He nodded. Our house felt like a perfectly working clock. We all turned at the right time and said the right things and maintained the same rhythm day in and day out without ever deviating. It was nice to have that routine. To feel grounded in something. Safe.

"Sit and tell me about prom last night."

"That's okay, you're in the middle of something."

He waved his hand at his sketchbook, the relaxed state he had been in moments before replaced with a straight back. "I'm nowhere near the middle. More like way past the end."

I sat in the chair across from him, knowing he wouldn't give up until I gave him a summary. And besides, it was time to tell him what he'd been wanting to hear for two months. "Bradley broke up with me."

His eyes went wide, then happy, then sympathetic, all in under a second. "At prom?"

I shrugged. "It's not a big deal."

"Do you need me to drive to UCLA and beat him up?"

I raised my eyebrows.

"You're right, he's way too big for me. I'll have your brother do it."

I gave him the laugh he was looking for then took a bite of my banana, knowing that even if my dad were being serious right now, Drew would never beat up anyone for me. We weren't close enough for that.

My dad folded his hands on the table. "Chin up. There are other fish in the sea. It's a big ocean. Sometimes we need to catch and release a few before we find the keeper. Just keep swimming."

"I don't think that last metaphor applies here."

"I was on a water roll. I just went with it."

I smiled then stood and threw away the banana peel. "All I ask is that you wait until I'm out of the house before you and Mom throw a party over this."

He gave me an overly serious nod as I left the room. There. That wasn't bad. I could now check off talking to my parents about the breakup from my list.

I went through the rest of the day in a haze, answering tweets about my newly single status and what parties were happening this weekend where I could celebrate. Bradley didn't respond to the tweet about being single. He'd probably unfollow me soon. I wondered if I should unfollow him first. I didn't.

That night I slept hard, thankful no dreams tried to remind me of prom.

School would be a good distraction, I thought as I jumped into the shower the next morning. I wasn't sure how long I stood under the water and it was possible I'd conditioned my hair twice. I picked out an outfit carefully, knowing I'd be on the other end of a lot of staring today, and stood in front of the mirror to get ready.

By the time I looked at my phone, I realized I'd spent way too much time perfecting my look. I'd have to skip breakfast. On my way through the kitchen I grabbed a granola bar.

"Running late, Mom," I called as her whole body turned to follow my path through the kitchen. Her wide eyes proved she was shocked I wasn't eating breakfast with her like I normally did. "I'll see you at five. We have a meeting after school."

"Okay. Love you."

"You too." I let the door swing shut behind me and threw my backpack onto the floorboard of the passenger seat before climbing into the car after it.

"Wow, you look good."

"Thanks."

Claire pointed to my front porch where my mom waved good-bye to us. I smiled and waved back.

"I swear your family should be on some Perfect Family billboard or something. What's it like to have the world's best parents?"

"They are pretty great. They always seem to do everything by the book."

"What book is that?"

"I don't know, *What to Say to Your Kids 101*?" I took a deep breath and opened my granola bar.

"You didn't eat breakfast?"

"No time."

Claire backed out of my driveway. "You okay? I didn't hear from you at all this weekend. I thought you'd want to go out last night."

I shrugged. "No, I had homework to finish."

"I'm sorry you didn't win."

"Win what?"

"Prom queen."

I gave a little laugh. "You think me not wanting to go out had to do with not winning prom queen?"

"I don't know, that or Bradley. I've just never seen you upset over a guy before."

I started to deny that staying home all weekend had to do with Bradley but in a weird way it did. Or at least with the person who'd filled in for him. He'd taken over my thoughts and was making it impossible to concentrate. Why was that the case when I hardly even knew him?

Maybe that was the point—that he had saved me the other night without knowing me at all. And I wanted to know why. "You're right. It does have to do with him."

"Is it because he basically broke up with you first by cheating on you?"

"What?"

"You're just always the breaker-upper. He beat you to it."

"I . . ."

She playfully punched my arm. "Don't deny it."

Bradley. He broke up with me. That tension in my chest was back at the thought of it. No, I was done with him. He'd left me in the parking lot at prom. He didn't get to make me feel bad anymore.

Claire grabbed my hand. "I'm sorry. I don't mean to make light of it. He pulled a jerk move. You should be upset. I should've taken you out for a milk shake or something." She squeezed my hand. "But you can't let a boy ruin your carefully crafted image. Pull yourself together and we'll mourn in private."

"Right. We wouldn't want that." Was this how I'd comforted her after Peter last year? "Did you guys have fun Saturday night after leaving prom? What did you end up doing?"

"We went over to the park and hung out. Tyler surfed on the swings."

"That sounds fun."

"It was funny. He almost ruined his tux."

I smiled. "So, Tyler? Are you feeling like you know him better now? He seemed nice."

She shrugged. "I don't know. He's a solid B, but I still think I have a chance with Logan. He's A material for sure. Don't you think?"

Logan. I vaguely remembered telling her a month ago when no one had asked her to prom yet that Logan was someone she should aim for. He was a star on the football team plus did well in school. But then Tyler had asked her and she seemed to like him so I thought she'd forgotten about Logan. Apparently not. "Logan had his chance. I think if you had a good time with Tyler that you should go for it."

"Not that it matters. We are leaving for college soon." She bit her lip, containing a smile. "Then we will have our pick of college boys. College men. Ones that are way better than Bradley."

"Right." I finished my granola bar and shoved the wrapper in my backpack.

"Oh, speaking of, my mom bought us a doormat."

"For our dorm?"

"Yes, I tried to tell her that our dorm was inside a building and it wasn't like an apartment, but she insisted."

"What does it look like?"

"Get this. It says, 'I am not a doormat.' " She groaned.

I laughed. "Do you think she is trying to send a message to our future visitors or just trying to be funny?"

"I don't think she gets the double meaning. I think she thinks the doormat is saying it's not a doormat and she finds that amusing."

"Your mom is funny."

"My mom is annoying."

"Between our two sets of parents, we're not going to have to buy anything for our dorm room."

She smiled and held up her fist for me to bump. "One hundred and three days until we're officially roommates."

"I can't wait."

We pulled into the parking lot at school. Right away I saw Laney and Jules heading our way from where they had just climbed out of the car. I braced myself. Jules had all weekend to analyze prom. Surely she'd come up with something incriminating.

CHAPTER 6

Laney and Jules joined us at the car.

"Gia," Laney said. "Tie breaker."

"Okay." I shouldered my backpack and shut the car door.

"Which building do you think is higher—the Holiday Inn or the Convention Center?"

"Um . . . what?"

"The boys were talking about rappelling off one. Hypothetically, of course."

"Which Holiday Inn? Beachfront or Downtown?"

"Beachfront."

"The Convention Center. Hands down. But Beach-front would be easier to rappel without getting caught."

"See?" Laney said, pointing at Jules.

"You act like Gia is the authority on building heights."

Great. I'd thought it was an argument between the boys. I hadn't realized I was going against Jules. It was like she was always on the opposing side from me whether I knew it or not. "But I could be wrong," I said. "I've never measured them." I walked toward campus, the others following after me.

"I'll Google it," Jules said.

She was constantly Googling things to prove she was right. The problem was that when she wasn't right she got all pissy, as if we had personally gone into Google and changed all the answers to go against her.

She pulled out her phone. "Oh, and while I'm online, I wanted to leave mean messages on Bradley's Facebook page for what he did to you. What's his last name again?"

Here it was—her play. I was surprised she had waited this long. "He isn't on Facebook. Who goes on Facebook anymore anyway?" He actually was on Facebook, but there was no way I was telling her that.

"So Instagram? Twitter? You showed me them before but I don't remember his handle," she pushed.

"We broke up, Jules. I don't want him to think I'm still hung up on him."

"But the messages will be from me." She held her phone poised like I was going to give her his social media information right there on the way to class. I wasn't sure if she thought she'd find something on one of those sites to incriminate me or if she knew he wasn't who I claimed him to be. "Did you see our prom picture I posted? It already has forty likes."

"Yes, I saw."

She handed me the phone anyway and I looked at the picture of the seven of us crowded around that table at prom. My date's head was mostly hidden by my own and I found myself wishing it wasn't. I held back a frustrated sigh over that thought and gave her back her phone.

"I've been thinking," Jules said.

Never a good thing, I thought.

"It's so weird that Bradley knew someone else from our school. Not only knew her but was having a relationship with her behind your back. What are the odds of that?"

Crap. Our story had holes. Big ones. Everyone seemed to analyze this statement because all their eyes were on me now to explain. One harmless lie. I thought that's all I'd have to tell that night at prom. I was just changing the order of events. And now here I was, still lying. I felt myself building the web and I was afraid the only one who was going to get trapped in it was me.

"He used to live here before I knew him. Before he went away to school. He must've known her from then."

"Who is she anyway?" Claire asked this time. "We should find her and talk to her. Tell her to stay away from Bradley."

"I didn't recognize her. Maybe she doesn't even go to school here. Maybe she went to prom with a friend." My anxiety was building, my heart racing. I didn't like lying. Lucky for me, Daniel Carlson sidestepped into our group, draping his arm around my shoulder. I was happy for the interruption, knowing he'd change the subject to student council stuff that we had been working on for the last few weeks. Or at least that's why I figured he was here. It's all we ever talked about anymore.

"So, now that you're single . . ."

Or maybe he wouldn't change the subject. "I don't do repeats, Daniel."

He laughed. "Too bad for you."

"Yes, it tears me up inside."

"So," he said. "Rally emergency. The sound system for the gym is down. Mr. Green doesn't know if it will be fixed by Friday."

"Okay, we'll discuss it at the meeting today."

"As vice president, I felt it important to report this

immediately as I am just a servant to your authority."

I hip-checked him. "Whatever. I'll see you after school."

"I'm dismissed, boss?"

I smiled. "Go away."

He ran off, joining another group of girls ahead of us. Claire and Laney had fallen a few steps behind, talking about calculus homework, but Jules was still at my side.

"I thought he said he didn't know our town very well. He asked if we had an arcade," Jules said.

I blinked, confused. "What?"

"Bradley. You said he lived here before, but he said he didn't know our town very well."

Something in me snapped. I wasn't going to put up with this anymore. I'd been trying to play nice for months now, thinking if I didn't they might choose her over me. But right now, I had to take the risk because I was tired of feeling like I had to defend myself every time I hung out with my best friends. So in a voice as low and stern as I could manage I said, "I'm done with this. You met Bradley. He's obviously real. If you continue to play whatever game it is that you're playing, I will take my friends and you will be gone."

My hands shook and I shoved them into my pockets so she couldn't see how upset it had made me to say that. I was assuming what I had told fill-in Bradley the other night was true—that she thought I was the leader of this group. If she thought that, this power play would work.

She narrowed her eyes and her head clicked one notch to the side, like a lioness assessing her next meal. "I'm not sure what you're talking about," her mouth said even though her look said, "Game on."

"Good. It was just my imagination, then." I took the steps to the C building quickly, outpacing the group. "See you guys at lunch."

A group good-bye echoed from the three of them and I ducked into the building while they continued on to the next one. I pressed my back against the wall, counted ten deep breaths until the shakiness was gone, then continued on to class.

I sank into my seat and the girl in front of me, a girl who normally sat on the other side of the room, turned around to pass me the quiz Mrs. Rios was already handing out.

"Thanks," I said, annoyed Mrs. Rios had chosen to give us a pop quiz on the Monday after prom. I pulled out my phone and quickly sent off a tweet: **PSA: Pop Quiz in Government.** That should win me a few points with my followers. It made me feel better to do something nice after what I'd just said to Jules. I sighed and tucked my phone away.

"Bad day?" the girl in front of me asked.

I met her eyes lined in thick black, like they always were, and gasped. It was fill-in Bradley's sister.

CHAPTER 7

"Bec?" I asked.

She just smirked at me then turned back around, retrieving a pencil from her backpack.

"That is so not fair," I said. "You looked nothing like this at prom." I gestured toward her outfit, which was black layered with more black, then to her face, which was covered in almost as much makeup as my makeup-hoarding grandma wore on bingo night.

"It was a social experiment. You failed." Bec paused. "Or succeeded in proving us right. Either way."

"So you're mad at me for not recognizing you when

you purposefully made it impossible."

"If that were your worst offense, I'd consider myself lucky."

I'd done something else to her? Something worse?

Mrs. Rios cleared her throat. "Girls, no talking. It's time for the quiz."

This morning had not started off well. Fill-in Bradley could've told me that his sister normally dressed like a heavy metal band member. I might've remembered her then. She'd only been here a few months—mid-year transfer. As far as I remembered, I hadn't said more than two words to her, so I wasn't sure what my other offenses might have been.

I was distracted for the entire quiz, my mind barely registering the questions let alone being able to answer them in an intelligent manner. I tried my best then stared at the back of Bec's head the rest of class waiting for my opportunity to talk to her. When the bell rang, I grabbed my backpack as quickly as she grabbed hers and matched her step for step out the door.

"What?" she barked when we were in the hall.

I wanted to ask what her brother's name was, but I couldn't admit that he hadn't told me. "I need your brother's phone number."

"Why?"

"I just wanted to send him a thank-you text." Right.

A thank-you text. It would go something like *Dear fill-in Bradley, Thank you for lying for me and tricking my friends by pretending to be my boyfriend. Now, can you tell me why you decided to come into prom with me? Why you wanted to help me? Why you gave me a super-intense look while we danced like you could see something in me that I had no idea existed? That way I can get you out of my head. Thank you.*

"If he wanted you to have his number, he would've given it to you." She seemed to take pleasure in saying this to me.

"He would've but he had to leave abruptly with the whole fake fight thing."

She groaned as if she had just remembered how I had used him again.

"If I give you my number, will you give it to him?"

"If I throw myself down these stairs, will you leave me alone?"

We had exited the building and were standing at the top of the cement stairs. A guy as equally punked-out as her stood at the bottom staring up at us. She didn't wait for my answer, which technically could've been yes or no, just walked down to join him.

"Hey, Gia," he said when I caught up with them both at the bottom.

I did a double take and realized he was the guy who

had been Bec's date to the prom. "Hi. I'm sorry. I don't know your name."

He shrugged. "I've only been in four of your classes over the last three years. Why would you?"

My cheeks reddened. Had he really? I looked at him again, closer. He honestly didn't look at all familiar to me, except from prom the other night. We did go to public school—class sizes were big.

"Watch out," Bec said, "your popular friends might see you walking with us."

I looked up to see Claire and Laney making a beeline for me. They probably wouldn't recognize her, but Bec was right, if they saw her and realized she was the same girl from prom, it would ruin everything. I changed my direction, leaving Bec and her boyfriend behind.

"Coward," Bec said when I was ten steps away. I tripped a little but didn't stop.

"Do you know them?" Laney asked when I met up with her and Claire.

"She's in my government class. We had a pop quiz. Who gives a pop quiz the Monday after prom? Our teacher is Satan, I've decided."

They didn't seem to notice that I'd completely glazed over their question, changing the subject. "Yeah, I saw your tweet. People were retweeting it all over the place."

"Gia!" a guy called out while walking by. "Thank you for the PSA. You're my hero."

Laney laughed.

Claire tugged on my arm, bringing my attention back to her. "Are you and Jules fighting again?"

Another question I wanted to glaze over. "She's been on my case about Bradley for two months and she still won't let it go."

"But we all met him. What could she possibly have to say now?"

My tongue felt two sizes too big for my mouth. Now was the time when I should come clean, tell them what she could dig up and how stupid I was for lying. That way she'd have nothing on me.

Laney grabbed my hand. "Just try to be nice to her. She's been through a lot."

"Right, it's just—" My phone chimed and I instinctively glanced at the screen.

Claire must've been looking over my shoulder because she said, "Don't you dare call him."

My eyes were still wide with shock. It was a message from Bradley: **I've been thinking about prom night . . . call me when you get home.**

I was home, staring at my phone, not calling Bradley. What I had told Daniel was true—I didn't do repeats.

But Claire was right too—I'd always been the one to break it off with a guy. The breakup with Bradley was sudden and I hadn't been prepared. Maybe it was premature. My mind tried to remind me that he had left me in the middle of the prom parking lot. I didn't want him back. But it wouldn't hurt to call him back, get better closure. Maybe if I told him how it felt to be left in the parking lot at prom, by myself, I'd feel better. Maybe it would help me get over this faster because I still got a stupid lump in my throat every time I thought of him.

I needed to touch Call. All the numbers were on the screen waiting for that simple act. What was stopping me? Nothing.

I touched the Call icon. My heart raced as the phone rang. I was going to do this. End it for good. Then why was I relieved when the call went to voice mail? "Heeey," his prerecorded message said. "You missed me. But I have your name and number on caller ID so unless I don't want to talk to you, I'll call you back." I laughed a little. Bradley was fun. It felt like I hadn't heard his voice in ages even though it had only been a couple of days. I pushed End without leaving a message then threw my phone on my bed and left it there while I spent the next few hours on homework.

When I went back to my room, my phone showed several missed texts from Claire and a missed call from

Bradley. I responded to the texts but I had made an important decision about Bradley. I had to wait to talk to him, give myself some time to calm down. I didn't want my emotions to tell a different story than my mind. In the meantime, I needed to see fill-in Bradley one more time. He needed to answer one simple question—why had he done it? He'd answer that question away from prom night, under normal circumstances. He'd be in his nerd T-shirt with his shaggy hair. Then I could be done with both the Bradleys and move on with my life.

This was my plan and I was determined to make it work. I started by opening my closet and retrieving my yearbooks from the top shelf.

CHAPTER 8

· · · · · · ·

My friends and I normally went off campus for lunch so it wasn't hard to stay behind claiming make-up testing. It also wasn't hard to find where Bec and her boyfriend hung out with a few other friends by the empty portables that were technically off limits during lunch.

I clutched the note with my phone number in my hand. I didn't want to admit how many times I had written my number so it looked the perfect amount casual, the perfect amount deliberate. I had never done that for a guy before. It added to my frustration over this whole situation. I just needed to talk to him, figure out his prom motivations, get him out of my head, and then it would be over.

Bec and another girl were playing tic-tac-toe in the dirt using sticks.

"Hi, Bec. Hi, Nate," I said when I approached. It had taken me two yearbooks and an hour and a half to figure out Nate's name but I did. He didn't seem impressed with my efforts. He just waved a half-eaten apple at me in greeting. Bec didn't even look up from her game.

I held up the note. "I was hoping you'd give this to . . ." I paused, praying that either Bec or Nate would provide me with a name.

Bec just looked up and said, "My brother?"

"Right. Will you give this to him for me?"

She filled in an X on the board in the dirt. "No."

"Please."

"Oh, well, since you asked nicely . . . no."

Her friend laughed. "Oh, look, it's Gia Montgomery. You told our friend his band sucked and that he should take up a new hobby."

I gasped. "I did not."

"Oh, that's right. Your friend Jules did and you laughed. Same difference."

I remembered that. It was the end of a very long day of bands trying out to play for prom. They were the fifth horrible band in a row and my head had been pounding.

Jules, who'd volunteered herself as one of the judges and had done a pretty good job of being nice, couldn't hold her comment in any longer. I did laugh. We all laughed. I shouldn't have. This was probably the "bigger offense" I'd committed that Bec had referred to the day before.

"Yeah . . . sorry about that. I had a headache."

"Don't apologize to me. It wasn't my dream you were crushing." She looked at Nate as if waiting for him to say something. Maybe she wanted him to get mad at me as well. He didn't.

"Right," I said. The hand, still clutching my ignored note, dropped to my side.

Bec drew a new empty board on the dirt, ignoring more than just my note. Nate took another bite of his apple and smiled at me but then shrugged as if to say, "You're out of luck."

"I'll see you tomorrow in class, then." I tucked the note into my jeans and left to the sounds of more laughter. I guessed it was okay when they were the ones doing the mocking.

"Can I take the car to school tomorrow?"

My mom's hand paused where it was reaching for a glass in the cupboard. "Why?" She grabbed the glass and turned to face me.

"I need to do something after school." *That may include*

following someone home like a creepy stalker. "I don't want to make Claire drive me."

She considered while she filled her glass with water from the door in the fridge. She was a real estate agent and if she had tons of appointments set up tomorrow it wouldn't work. But she usually wasn't too busy on weekdays. The weekends were when people needed to look at the twelfth house they wouldn't buy or the one they'd already looked at twelve times. "That should be fine. I can borrow Dad's car if I need it, but this isn't going to be the norm, right? You and Claire aren't fighting or anything? Dad told me about Bradley."

Her thought progression made no sense to me. Was she saying that because I'd fought with Bradley, I must be fighting with everyone I knew? "No, we're fine. We're . . . the same as we've always been." Everything in my life was the same as it had always been. I may have felt off, but everything around me was exactly the same.

"Good. You'd hate to start college fighting with your roommate."

"Uh . . . thanks, Mom."

She laughed. "You know what I mean."

I knew what she meant and she was right, I didn't want that to happen. Why had I lied to Claire? "Yes, you're right. But we're not fighting." At least not yet. I watched her drink her water and thought about asking her what she thought the result of lying to my friends would be. Maybe she'd have some insights. But I didn't ask.

"Thanks for letting me use the car," I said, then left the kitchen.

I dialed Claire's number as I walked the hall to my room. I fell back on my bed. "Hi, Claire," I said when she answered.

"Hey."

"So I don't need a ride tomorrow to school. I'm using my mom's car."

"Why?" It was a fair question. We'd been riding to school together since we got our licenses and my parents had made the executive decision that I didn't need my own car. I blamed my brother for the three accidents he had gotten into before he turned eighteen. The only time I didn't ride with Claire was when one of us was sick.

"I have to run some errands for my mom." The lies were endless at this point and it sucked. I sucked.

"Are you mad at me?"

"Of course not."

"It's just, you've been acting weird since prom."

I'd felt weird since prom, like maybe for the first time I was really evaluating my life and discovering I came up lacking. Starting with the fact that Bec was right—I was a coward. I was scared to tell my friends the truth. What if Claire didn't want to room with me at college? What if she hated me? "I know, I'm sorry."

"It's okay." She gave a little sigh.

I steered the conversation back to a safer topic. "Do you believe we're about to graduate?"

"I know, high school seemed to take forever and now it's speeding by."

I twisted the corner of my sheet around my finger over and over and listened to her talk about how fun college was going to be. Yes, finding fill-in Bradley was key. He had done this to me and I needed it undone.

It had all gone as planned so far. I'd been able to discreetly find Bec after school where she got into the passenger seat of a car that did not belong to her brother. Well, it could've, but he wasn't driving it. We'd made two right turns and passed three stoplights. He'd said he lived only six blocks from the school, so I imagined we were coming close to their house. My palms started to sweat, so I wiped them on my jeans, keeping my eyes on the taillights in front of me. I couldn't lose them. Their car's blinker went on and so did mine. Then they turned into the parking lot of a 7-Eleven. I hesitated, not wanting to lose them, but it was a small parking lot. Bec would surely see me.

I started to pass but decided at the last second not to and turned the wheel, causing the tires to squeal. I cringed, sure they heard, but it didn't matter, they were already out of their car and Bec was standing there waiting for me.

I sighed and parked next to them.

"Are you following us?"

"What? No. It's half-off Slurpee day," I said, reading the sign in the window. "I always come here on Wednesdays."

She glanced over her shoulder at the door then back to me. "Really? Huh. Well, we just thought you were following us. Guess not. Enjoy your Slurpee." She reached for the handle.

"Wait. You're not going inside?"

"No."

"You're going home?"

"Yes."

She opened the car door.

"Fine, I never come here on Wednesdays. I was following you," I blurted out. "I just want to see him again."

She leaned her hip against the door and gave me a slow once-over. "Yeah, not happening." And with that she got into the car and they drove away.

Since when did I chase things? This was pointless. I was done. I didn't need to find him to forget him. It was over. I was moving forward. A big weight lifted off my shoulders with that thought. One Bradley down, one to go.

CHAPTER 9

His outgoing message ended, followed by the loud beep. I took a breath and said, "Hey, Bradley, it's me. Call me back when you get a minute." I wasn't going to tell him in a voice mail that I wasn't regretting our breakup.

I pressed End and threw the phone on the passenger seat. When I pulled up to my house, Claire's car sat out front and she sat in it, waiting for me.

"Hey," I said as we both stepped out of our cars.

She held up a cup. "A few days late, but here it is."

I joined her. "What is it?"

"A milk shake."

I smiled and gave her a hug, holding on for a couple of seconds too long before pulling away. "You're the best. Let's go inside."

"I can't, I'm going surfing. Wanna come?"

I laughed. "Are you going to ask me that every time you go? It's as though you like to hear me say no."

She smiled. "I just feel like you're missing out on one of the true joys in life."

"What's that? Super-freezing water, gross salty hair, and washing away sand for days?"

"Well, when you put it like that, it sounds bad."

"Exactly."

She swatted my arm. "It's fun. Peaceful."

"You know what's also fun and peaceful? Drinking a shake." I took a big sip from mine.

"That's true. Or eating brownies."

"Or pedicures."

"Naps."

"Music."

"Guys," we both said at the same time then laughed.

Well, normally guys are, I thought. Not so much lately.

"We are so the same person," she said. "Well, except for that surfing thing."

"Yeah, come on, get past that so we don't have this wedge between us."

My smile turned a little forced as I thought about the

only wedge between us and who had put it there.

"So how did your make-up tests go yesterday?"

"Make-up tests?" I remembered one moment too late that she was talking about the excuse I'd used to stay behind on campus and talk to Bec. "Yeah, they went well. . . ."

"That doesn't sound like they really did. Are you worried you're failing something?"

Our friendship. I couldn't tell any more lies. I was turning over a new leaf, starting fresh. "I wasn't taking a make-up test."

"Okay . . . what were you doing?"

"I had to talk with someone on campus."

"Who?"

"Her name is Bec. I just didn't want the whole gang coming. She hangs out by the portables."

"With the stoners?"

"I'm pretty sure they're not stoners."

"Well, they act like—" Her phone chimed and she stopped mid-sentence to check it. "They're waiting for me. I probably better go."

"Who's waiting for you?"

"Jules and Laney. Remember, I told you we're surfing."

"I thought you were surfing by yourself, peacefully."

She laughed. "No, they wanted to come this time."

"Jules surfs?"

She shrugged. "She wants to learn."

It took everything in me not to run inside and put my suit on like I now wanted to. I wasn't going to change my mind just because the three of them would be there without me. And I also wasn't going to rush telling her about prom right now. I'd tell her when she had more time. "Have fun."

As Claire got in her car I yelled out, "Thanks for this," and held up my shake.

"May it bring you peace," she said with a smile, then drove away.

In Government the next morning as I sat down, Bec immediately turned around in her seat. "Change of plans. It's time to pay up."

"Uh . . . what?"

"You owe my brother a favor and I'm here to collect."

She wanted me to do something for her brother when I'd just banned him from my brain? "I can't."

"You owe him." She pulled something out of her bag and slapped it onto my desk. It was an envelope, its top edge jagged.

"What is it?" I asked without picking it up.

"It's not going to bite you."

"And you didn't poison it?"

"Open it."

I picked it up and took out the single page inside. An invitation, printed on gold-bordered paper. "Are you inviting me to your birthday party?"

"You're just a regular comedian this morning, aren't you?"

I read the invitation. *You're invited to a graduation party for Eve Sanders. Saturday, May 7th at 7pm.* "Am I supposed to know who this is?"

"My brother's ex."

My eyes zeroed in on the address included on the invite. Eve lived only, like, twenty minutes away. Bec and her brother had moved from across town?

Bec continued, "I found it on the counter last night and then I heard him calling her to confirm that he is actually going to that thing. She invited him. And he is going. She's trying to sink her claws into him again when she is the one who left him. She is awful, Gia. Worse than you."

"Thanks."

"You're just clueless. She's intentionally mean."

"Was that supposed to make it better?"

The bell rang and Mrs. Rios stood in front of the class, her eyes narrowing in on me. Bec turned around to face the front. My attention drifted to the invitation still on my desk. When Mrs. Rios turned to write something on the whiteboard, I leaned forward. "So, I don't under-stand. What do you want me to do about this?"

Mrs. Rios must have supersonic hearing because her head whipped toward us. I leaned back. Half of class passed and I swore Bec was just trying to drive me insane by not saying a word. Finally she slipped a note back to me.

You are going to be his date to the party. His new "girl-friend." You owe him.

My heart thumped loud in my chest. I had told him I owed him a fake date on prom night. He'd taken me up on it. Why had he taken me up on it?

The day passed excruciatingly slowly as I thought about Saturday. I hoped seeing him again wasn't going to screw up my plans. No, this was good. Like I said before, he could answer my questions and it would be over.

It was hot as I headed toward Claire's car at the end of the day. Had it been this hot all day? I peeled off my sweater and laced it through the strap of my backpack. When I looked up, Logan Fowler was standing in front of me, blocking my path. His easy smile and confident posture reminded me why I had told Claire to ask him to prom. He was definitely A material. I returned his smile.

"Logan."

"Gia. What happened at prom? You were supposed to be my queen."

"Are you rubbing it in that you won and I didn't, Logan?"

He let out a loud laugh. "I was just surprised you didn't, that's all."

Why did everyone else keep bringing this up? Did they want me to be upset? "I guess you'll have to dance with me another time." I moved to go around him but he held out his arm, stopping me.

"I'm having a party this weekend. Come."

"This weekend?"

"Saturday."

The invitation that Bec had left sitting on my desk for all of first period flashed in my mind. Of course it would be the same day. She'd kill me if I bailed now. "I can't, but thanks for the invite." I pushed his arm away and left him, throwing a smile over my shoulder to let him know I wasn't trying to be mean.

"I see how you are. Playing hard to get."

I laughed and kept walking.

Claire was already in her car when I got there. I collapsed into the passenger seat.

"Well, hello to you too," Claire said.

"Hey, baby."

"Oh, now you talk sweet to me." She started the car. "So, check out my hair."

I looked at her hair but didn't see anything out of the ordinary. It was long and black and shiny just like it always was. "Yep, it's still perfect."

She shoved my shoulder. "I want you to note that there are still no aftereffects of surfing yesterday. No— how do you put it? —saltwater trauma."

"Well, that's because you have beautiful magic Asian hair. Mine wouldn't be as kind."

"Magic Asian hair?"

"Don't try to deny it. How did it go yesterday? Did you all have fun?"

"We did, but Jules and her mom are fighting again so it turned into a therapy session."

"Did you tell her that no one gets along with their mom?"

"Except you."

"You didn't tell her *that*, did you?" As if Jules needed another reason to hate me.

"No, I didn't. But her issues with her mom go beyond the norm and there really wasn't much I could say that made her feel better."

"What's going on? Is she okay?"

"I really don't feel like it's my place to tell you. Maybe you could try talking to her."

"She doesn't want to talk to me. And what makes you think I'd be able to help?"

"I don't know. You're good with people."

"Not with her." Claire was probably just trying to get Jules and me to talk more. She'd probably given Jules some story about me as well that she was supposed to help me with. But Jules didn't want to be my friend so I wasn't sure why Claire thought anything I said to her would make a difference. I knew it meant a lot to Claire, though, and maybe it really would help so I said, "I'll try."

"Thank you."

The first thing I noticed when Claire pulled up to my house was my brother's beat-up car sitting at the curb.

"Drew's here?" Claire said. "I should probably stay."

"Funny," I said. "And gross."

"Come on, you know he's cute. I can't help it." She turned off her car and got out with me. I rolled my eyes but laughed.

Inside, Drew had a plate piled with food like he hadn't eaten in weeks. Maybe the last good meal he had was here, three weeks ago. He had some new growth on his face that made him seem so much older than me when really we were only three years apart.

"You're home," I said unnecessarily.

His mouth was full of food but he smiled anyway. He even added a "Hey, sis."

"Hi."

"Hi," Claire said as well.

He swallowed. "How's it going? And yes, I'm home for the weekend."

"It's only Thursday."

"I don't have classes on Fridays."

I wondered if his being here would change my plans for Saturday. Would Mom want us to have some sort of family dinner that night?

Claire sat down at the table in the chair across from him. "How is UCLA? I'll be there in a hundred days with Gia."

He gave her an amused look. "And how many hours?"

Her cheeks went pink. "I don't have that figured out."

"Well, you'll love it. It's great." Drew took another bite of food then he turned toward me. "I ran into Bradley the other day."

"Oh?" My face went numb. I didn't want to talk about Bradley right now, in front of Claire. I was worried something might come out. When I told Claire the truth, it needed to be just her and me. My brother wouldn't help.

"He said you guys are fighting?"

"That's what he said? That we're *fighting*?" I wasn't sure what that meant. That he thought we might get back together? He hadn't called me back since I left the message the day before.

Drew's brows went down. "I think that's what he said. Are you not fighting?"

"He broke up with me."

"He cheated on her," Claire added.

Crap. "Well, I mean, that's what it seemed like," I said to smooth things over in case my brother relayed this back to Bradley.

"What do you mean that's what it seemed like?" Claire said, indignant on my behalf. "There was that other girl there. He basically admitted to it."

"Right. But we didn't see anything and I haven't really let him explain."

"You're going to forgive him?" Claire asked, standing to face me.

"No." It was nearly impossible to convey two different things at the same time. I couldn't let my brother go back to Bradley with the cheating story, but I didn't want Claire to think I was getting back together with him after he "cheated" on me.

"Huh," my brother said. "I hadn't heard that side of the story."

"What did you hear?" I asked, unable to contain my curiosity about how Bradley was telling the story.

"He just said you had a fight and he'd been trying to call you. He asked how you were. I said I hadn't talked to you in a while but that according to Twitter you were . . . um . . . how did you put it? 'Chillin' at home'?"

"You really said that to him?"

"That's what you wrote on Twitter. You're okay with the world reading it but not Bradley?"

"The world doesn't read my Twitter," I mumbled.

"Do you want me to find out if he's cheating on you? I have connections." He said this in a mob-boss kind of voice.

"No," I said, but Claire said, "Yes" right over me.

He looked between the two of us.

"No," I said again. "Please, I don't need my brother policing my relationship."

He leaned into the table. "Gia, I hope you're not trying to pretend everything is fine if a guy cheated on you. You should be pissed about that."

"I am. I mean, I would be if he really had."

Claire's mouth dropped open at this point. Drew shook his head. "Claire, in case you haven't learned this about my sister, everything in her world is perfect. Even if it really isn't."

I had almost forgotten how Drew was. He liked to stir

up trouble. It was like he lived for it. He got some sick, manic pleasure from it.

"You've at least talked to the parents about this, right? Or *someone*?" He looked at Claire with his last sentence.

"Claire was there that night. And yes, Mom and Dad know we broke up."

"And I'm sure you had a real heart-to-heart about it. Dad told you some overused metaphors, Mom told you not to stir up trouble, and you smiled like they are the best parents in the world."

"Stop it." I wanted to get along with my brother, but the only thing he wanted to do was make me feel bad about myself.

"Or what?" He smiled at me.

"Just don't. Please."

He held up his hands. "Fine, I'll stay out of it."

"Thank you."

He put his plate in the sink. "Gotta do some laundry. We'll catch up more later."

When he was gone, Claire said, "You're not really thinking about getting back together with Bradley, are you?"

"No?"

She shook her head. "That doesn't exactly sound like conviction. Don't let his dreamy blue eyes and perfect smile make you forget what he did."

I felt my face wrinkle into confusion before I remembered she was describing my fill-in date. I nearly laughed at her description. He did have dreamy blue eyes and a perfect smile. And was too skinny and had shaggy hair. "Right. I won't forget what he did."

CHAPTER 10

•   •   •   •   •   •   •

I was a ball of nerves. What was I supposed to wear to a graduation party where I was playing the fake girl-friend? I called Claire and Laney over to help me pick out an outfit, trying to keep the same pre-date routine I always had.

Carrying a Coke Freeze, Claire walked into my room and sat down in my desk chair. Laney took the bed next to the clothes I'd laid out. "Are these the top choices so far?"

"Yes." I grabbed the first outfit, a pair of shorts and a flowy blouse, and went to my closet to change.

"Where's Jules?" Claire asked.

"She said she couldn't come." I'd told Claire I'd try, and even though I hadn't really wanted her to come over, I'd called and invited Jules.

"I talked to her on the way over."

"Oh, good. Did she change her mind?"

"She said you didn't invite her."

I came out of the closet half dressed. "She said what? I called her and told her to come. How is that not inviting her?"

Claire sighed as if she didn't know who to believe. "You guys need to get used to each other or you'll never survive next year."

I started to continue arguing about inviting her but then stopped. "Wait, what?"

"Next year . . . college."

"She . . ." I didn't even want to finish that sentence.

"Yes, she got into UCLA. She didn't tell you?"

She was too busy sabotaging me. "No, she didn't." I slunk back into the closet to put my shirt on. This was not good news. It made my insides burn. I tried to push that feeling away and walked back out, holding my hands to the sides. "Yes?"

"No," Laney said. "Too casual." She threw me the yellow sundress.

Claire said, "She said she was going to tell you."

"This is the first I'm hearing of it. But that's great," I said from in the closet because I wasn't sure if my face would support my words. "It should be fun." I really did have to fix something, because there was no way I wanted to continue this drama in college. "Now I really wish you were coming too, Laney."

"I know. Don't remind me. Community college is sounding worse and worse every day."

"It's not too late to join us," Claire said.

"Actually I'm about four years' worth of good grades and thousands of dollars too late for UCLA."

"Who needs money and good grades when you have community college?" Claire said.

"Exactly what I've been saying for the last four years," Laney said. I could hear the embarrassment in her voice and I felt bad that school had been a struggle for her.

I pulled the dress over my head, straightened it, then joined them in my room. "You'll have fun, Laney. And we're only three hours away. We'll see each other all the time."

She folded the outfit I had already tried on and smoothed the shirt over and over. "You hardly saw Bradley at all and he was your boyfriend."

"Exactly. He was just my boyfriend. You've been my

83

best friend for five years. It will be way different."

Claire joined Laney on the bed and wrapped her up in a hug. "Who needs a Laney sandwich?"

I rushed over to hug her from the other side.

"It's fine, guys. Don't feel sorry for me."

"We don't feel sorry for you. We just needed a hug." I squeezed her tighter.

She laughed. "I'm going to miss you."

I gave her one last squeeze then stood up.

"I think that's the outfit," Laney said.

I let her change the subject, sensing she needed to. "You think? Does it say backyard barbecue?" I did a turn. "It even has pockets for my cell phone."

"I'm so confused. Who is this new guy? I can't get over the fact that you haven't told us anything about him." Claire reached for her drink still sitting on the desk and nearly fell off the bed.

Laney grabbed her leg, preventing the fall. "Yes, don't we get to know?"

"It's a blind date. I don't know anything about him."

"Who is setting you up on a blind date and since when have you ever agreed to go out with someone sight unseen?"

I flinched. I'd never been set up on a blind date before, but I assumed I would've said yes if I trusted the person setting me up. "This girl in my government class. She's a junior. It's her older brother."

"What? Some girl from your class set you up with her brother and you said yes?"

"I kind of owe her a favor."

"Why?"

"I haven't been very nice to her and her friends."

"Oh, I get it. This is like a charity date? Are you going to be safe?"

"No. I mean, yes, of course I'll be safe. And no, her brother is not in need of charity." I turned and looked at myself in the full-length mirror. "So yes? No?"

"Yes, it's perfect. Wear your hair down and wavy and pair it with your wedge sandals. Unless he's short. Is he short?"

"No, he's not short." He was actually a really good height for me. "So, are you guys going to Logan's party tonight?"

Claire, who had been stirring her straw around her cup, looked up. "Logan's having a party tonight?"

"Yes."

"We hadn't heard about it," Laney said.

"Oh, sorry. I should've told you. I thought he was just inviting everyone. You should go."

"We weren't invited."

"He probably figured I'd tell you. Sorry."

Claire and Laney met eyes for a brief second and then

Claire went back to her drink. "Yeah, that sounds like fun. Maybe we should go, Laney. Let's invite Jules too."

I couldn't tell if they were mad at me for not telling them or what. I felt bad. I'd just figured he was telling everyone. "I'll try to join you all after my date."

My mom was trying to be polite; I could tell by the smile on her face. The problem was it was the most forced smile ever and there was no way Bec couldn't tell.

"Where are you going again?" my mom asked, looking mostly at me but her eyes kept darting to Bec, this time lingering on the row of earrings that lined her left ear.

"Just to my house. We have Government together and Gia said she would help me study. Here's the address." Bec slid a piece of paper across the counter to my mom. "And my parents' phone number is on there too if you need to talk to them." She smiled and my mom's smile became a little less forced.

But to me my mom said, "Your brother is in town. I wanted us to go out to dinner tonight as a family."

Just as she said this, Drew walked through the kitchen holding his car keys. "I'm going out with some friends, Mom. Can we do dinner next time I'm in town?"

"What?" my mom asked.

Drew stopped in the middle of the kitchen when he

saw Bec, a look of curiosity taking over his expression. He took in both her outfit then mine and didn't need to say anything out loud for me to know he was wondering who Bec was and why she was here.

"This is Gia's friend," my mom said. "Bec, right?"

"You two are friends?" His tone conveyed his disbelief.

Bec let out a single laugh. "Not so much friends as study partners."

This explanation didn't change Drew's expression. He looked at me like he was seeing me for the first time. "Huh," he grunted, then finished walking through the kitchen. "We good, Mom?" He flashed her the smile I remembered always got him out of the trouble he'd caused when he lived here.

She shooed him away with a smile of her own.

I pointed toward the front door. "See, he's not even staying. So I can go, right?"

"How come you're so dressed up for a study session?" Mom asked, looking me up and down.

The excuse came easy. "Because she has a cute brother."

My mom rolled her eyes as if she now understood the whole reason I was hanging out with this strange creature standing in her kitchen. "Okay, keep your cell phone on, Gia."

"Of course." I kissed her cheek and Bec and I left my house silently.

When we got outside, I said, "Why the need for an elaborate story? I thought your brother would pick me up."

"Obviously not."

"It's just I didn't prepare my mom for . . ."

"Me?"

"Yeah."

"Well, parents love the 'she's helping me study' thing. It makes them think their kid is smart. But for the record, my grade in Government is two percentage points higher than yours. So if you need help studying . . ."

I laughed.

"Is she going to be pissed that you went out when she was planning on going to dinner as a family?"

"I don't think she'd been planning on it necessarily." I mostly thought she was using that as an excuse not to let me go with Bec.

"So she always looks like that?"

"Like what?" I glanced over my shoulder expecting to see her standing on the porch, but it was empty.

Bec unlocked the car doors and we climbed in. "Perfectly put-together."

I thought about my mom, her hair always styled, her makeup always done. I'd rarely seen her any other way. "Yeah . . . I guess so."

As Bec backed out of the driveway my mother appeared on the porch. I smiled and waved. "So when my mom calls your parents, because she most likely will, they're going to be okay?"

"I gave her *my* phone number."

"Oh. Right." Other kids probably tricked their parents like that all the time but I'd never had to. "So wait, if you can drive, why did your brother have to drop you off at prom?"

"Because supposedly he needed the car that night, which was another reason I was so angry to see him at prom with you."

"What was he supposed to be doing?"

"I have no idea." She pulled away from my house. It was the moment of truth. I was about to see fill-in Bradley again.

CHAPTER 11

When we got to her house, Bec ushered me inside and straight into her bedroom, closing the door. Had this been some sort of elaborate plan to murder me? I did a full circle, taking in a room that didn't seem like it belonged to her. Well, some of it did—like the band posters of boys wearing guyliner and the roughly sketched charcoal pictures. But then there were beautiful photographs of nature—a wave breaking against a rock, the canopy of a tree, a cloud-filled sky. On her dresser was a big vase full of colorful sea glass.

"That's what you're wearing to the barbecue?" she

asked, forcing my attention back to her. She was staring at my shoes.

I looked down at my outfit in a panic before I remembered who I was taking fashion advice from. "It got the three-girl vote of approval."

She sighed. "Okay, whatever. My brother will probably love it. You look . . ." She waved her hand at my outfit as if that counted as an adjective. "So anyway, here's how this is going to work."

"Wait. What do you mean how it's going to work?"

"What I'm going to tell him."

"He doesn't know?" I practically yelled.

"Shh." She looked back at the door then shook her head twice. Here I'd thought he had been the mastermind behind this plan and that Bec had reluctantly arranged it but he didn't want this at all. Great, he was going to think I wanted him or something when all he really wanted was his old girlfriend back. It was Bec who didn't. "Believe me, he will be happy that he doesn't have to go alone."

"He'd better be or I'm out of here."

"Oh, no you aren't. You owe him and even if he doesn't know this is for the best, you have to help me convince him that it is."

"You want me to help you convince him?"

"Only if he needs convincing. Now wait here while

I talk to him." She left the room, closing the door softly behind her.

There was no way I was waiting here and going into this blind. I needed to know what he thought of this whole thing. I cracked the door just in time to see her disappear around the corner then I followed her.

I pressed my back against the wall at the end of the hall and listened.

"Hey, Bec, what's up." At fill-in Bradley's voice my mind was able to conjure up the perfect image of him—blue eyes, brown hair, tall, a defined jawline.

"Looks like you're going somewhere," Bec said.

"I am."

"I know where you're going."

I could almost hear his eyebrow raise.

"And I don't think it's a smart idea."

"Have you been snooping in my mail?"

"She treated you like crap and then cheated on you and you're going to give her the satisfaction of seeing you show up at her party dateless and alone."

"How do you know I'm not taking a date?"

I let out a small gasp of surprise. He'd already fig-ured this out without our help. He had claimed on prom night that he would never be in need of a fake date. It was obviously true. Bec wouldn't even have to reveal that I was here if he really was going with a date. She'd probably be happy that he'd found someone so he didn't have to take me.

"Oh, please. You don't have a date. You've been a recluse since she broke up with you."

He laughed and my heart returned to beating a normal rhythm. "Are you trying to go to the party with me, Bec? If you want to go, all you have to do is ask."

"No, I'm not. Me being there would do nothing for you. What I want is for you to show up confident with proof that you have moved on from that horrible girl."

"She's not horrible."

"I think time has made you forget the extent of her betrayal."

His voice went low. "I haven't forgotten."

"Then why are you going? Why?"

"I guess I need some closure."

"And you can't talk to her at school or something?"

"I haven't seen her at school lately. She goes off campus for lunch. I'm not going to hunt her down."

"And yet here you are . . . hunting her down."

"Getting closure."

"Only that's not what is going to happen. I know her. She would only invite you for two reasons. One, she wants to rub in your face how happy she is with he-who-will-not-be-named and make sure you haven't moved on. Or two, she's dumped him and realized how great you are and wants you back. I'm pretty sure it's the second, and I think you might just be crazy enough to take her back."

"I'm not going to take her back."

"You're right. You're not because I found a date for you. Not just any date, a gorgeous one who will pretend to be in love with you."

"You hired me an escort?"

Bec laughed. "That was my backup plan."

There was silence for a moment then he said, "You're serious, aren't you? You really did get me a date for this."

"Yes, I'm very serious. She's here right now."

"Bec! No. This is not happening. Tell the poor girl she can go home."

"She's not a poor girl. She knows why she's here."

"And she agreed?"

"Yes, she owes you a favor."

"She owes me a favor . . . ?"

He obviously hadn't been thinking about me as much as I had about him because with a clue like that he should've immediately known it was me.

Bec cleared her throat. "I know you're in the hall so you might as well come out."

How did she know I was in the hall? Also, I didn't want to step out now because I felt beyond stupid. I just wanted to go home . . . after I asked him why he went to prom with me.

"Hello? Time to come out. You promised."

I swallowed and stepped out from behind the wall.

Fill-in Bradley's eyes went wide and he took me in from head to toe. "Gia?" His head whipped to his sister. "Gia?"

"Yes. Gia," she said. "You're welcome."

"You know I had nothing to do with this." He tugged on the bottom of a T-shirt that said, *You can't take the sky from me.* His hair needed my help again, but he was cuter than I remembered.

"Yes. Well, I know . . . now."

"You do not have to come with me. You look amazing, really amazing, but I'd actually rather go by myself, no offense."

"None taken." Technically I hadn't wanted to go with him to this stupid party where I wouldn't know anyone either, but his saying he didn't want me to go was a little jab to the gut. He'd rather go by himself than have to take me? Whatever. It didn't matter. If I left right now I could go to Logan's party with my friends. "I should probably just go home."

"Yes," fill-in Bradley said at the same exact time Bec said, "No!"

I looked between the two of them. Bec's eyes were pleading. I had told her I'd try to convince him, plus I kind of agreed with her. He shouldn't be going to his ex's party alone. *Especially* if he was trying to win her back.

"Listen, I don't have to pretend to be your girlfriend or anything. I could just go as your friend."

"I really don't want to make you do that."

"You wouldn't be making me. Plus I got all dressed up."

He smiled. "We wouldn't want that to go to waste."

"Right?"

"Good," Bec said. "It's settled." Then she grabbed my arm and pulled me back toward her room before he could object any more. "I just need to talk to Gia for a second and then she'll be ready."

"Okay," he said.

When we were in her room, she turned to me. "Good call on the friends thing. That will get you there, then once you're there you can hold his hand and kiss his cheek and whatever other girlfriend stuff you need to do to pull this off."

"Bec, I was serious about the friend thing. It wasn't a ploy. It's so obvious he wants his ex back."

"You see that too?"

"Yes." He may have been claiming some closure thing, but it was obvious.

I picked up my purse from where I had left it on the floor of her bedroom. "At least he's agreed to let me go, right?" On her dresser as I was leaving the room I saw several bottles of hair product. "I'm borrowing one of these." I held up a small tube of gel and shoved it in my purse.

"Do your job," she said as I left. "It's not too late to save him from her."

I was not going to force my fake girlfriendness on anyone tonight, so I just laughed and went to find fill-in Bradley.

CHAPTER 12

I pulled the seat belt across my chest and clicked it in place. "Did you know that your sister never uses your first name? It's just 'my brother this' and 'my brother that.' It's maddening."

He laughed a loud laugh that made me smile, then he pulled out of the driveway and onto the road.

"It's actually really cute. I think that's how she thinks of you always, as her big brother."

His amused look softened. "So you still don't know my name?"

"No. And I need it for tonight."

He didn't provide me the answer but instead asked, "What have you been calling me in your head, then?"

"What makes you think you've been in my head?"

He just smirked like he knew he had. And he was right.

"Fill-in Bradley."

He laughed. "Wow. Creative."

"It's all I had to work with so help me out here."

"Here's the problem. There's this huge buildup now. I almost feel like I need to make up a name that fits this moment of anticipation."

I gave him a stare of impatience. "Spit it out, fill-in Bradley, or that's what you're going to be from here on out."

"Do you realize the acronym for fill-in Bradley is FIB? It's kind of ironic, right?"

I smacked his arm playfully several times while saying, "Tell me your name."

He laughed and grabbed my hand, pushing it down onto the center console then trapping it there with his. "My name is . . ."

"You're right, this is super climactic. I don't think there is anything you can possibly say that will match the anticipation I feel right now."

"You're not helping."

"Should I guess?"

"We have about fifteen minutes, so you might as well."

"Okay, let's play Twenty Questions."

"All right. Hit me. Not literally, though." He squeezed my hand then let it go.

I smiled. "First question. Were you named after anyone famous?"

"Hmm. Well, yes and no. I mean, there are famous people with my name but I was named after someone not so famous with my name."

I tilted my head at him. "Really? You have to be confusing like that?"

"Is that one of your questions?"

"No, if you're going to be so strict with the rules, it's not. My next question is, can your name also be a last name or close to a last name?"

"What do you mean 'close to a last name'?"

"Like by adding a letter or something. William isn't necessarily a last name, but Williams is. Phillip to Phillips. Edward to Edwards. You get it."

"I do."

"Then there are the unmodified last names that can also be first names, like Taylor, Scott, Carter, Thomas, Lewis, Harris, Martin, Morris—"

"You think my name is Morris?"

"Just an example."

"You sure think about names a lot. Wait, don't tell

me, you're one of those girls who's already named all her future children."

"No, I'm not." Well, not *all* of them.

"That's good. And yes, my name can be a last name."

"A modified one?"

"No."

"A common one?"

"Not so much."

I pursed my lips to the side, thinking. "Is it a name that can also double as a word?"

"Explain."

"You know, like Hunter or Forest or Stone—"

"Or Tree?"

"Ha-ha. No, I was going to say Grant. As in, grant me the patience to deal with this boy while I am trapped in a car with him."

"Trapped? I seem to recall you practically begging to come with me."

"I don't beg."

With this he let out one big laugh.

"Okay, fine, I begged on prom night but whatever." I hit him again. Then something occurred to me. "So why were you waiting in the parking lot anyway? You live six blocks from the school and your sister has a cell phone. Plus your sister said you had somewhere to be."

He was quiet for so long that I thought maybe I'd

brought up a sore subject. Finally he said, "If I tell you, I don't want you to think I'm some sort of creep."

"I make no promises."

"I was worried about you."

"About *me*?"

"I pulled in right as Bradley had unlinked your arms from his waist and pushed you away. Then you were yelling at each other. And the look on your face after he left . . . I just wanted to make sure you were okay and that you had a ride home. I pulled out a book so I didn't look too creepy while waiting to see what you were going to do."

Two feelings competed to take over my emotions. The first was extreme embarrassment at how pathetic I must've looked. The second was appreciation at how nice he had been without even knowing me. The gratitude won. "Thank you," I said. "That's very . . ."

"Creepy?"

"No, sweet. So is that why?"

"Why, what?"

"You said it wasn't my smile that got you to go to prom with me but something else. Was it that you felt sorry for me?"

"Maybe a little at first, but then, you looked so . . ."

"Hot?" I prompted when he didn't finish.

He smiled. "So lonely."

The smile that had been on my face with the joke slipped off. "Lonely?"

He didn't respond.

"I have a lot of friends."

"Don't be mad. It was just an observation. I was probably wrong."

"You are wrong." Here I'd thought he'd seen something in me that I hadn't known I possessed, something he had figured out about me. It was the main reason I'd wanted to find him. Nobody had ever looked at me with the intensity that he had that first night. Nobody had ever seemed to see inside of me, beyond the obvious. But really he just felt sorry for me. He didn't know me at all. Why wasn't I at Logan's party right now?

"Okay, I'm sorry. But good thing I felt that way or you wouldn't have had a fake boyfriend that night."

"True."

He ran a hand through his hair and threw me a big-eyed look as if to apologize again. It helped. "My name. It can't double as a word, no."

Right, back to the game. "Okay, so it's not a super-famous person, it could be a last name but not a very common one, and it can't be used in a sentence. This is hard."

"Well, there are only a million names, so yeah. . . ."
He had a nice smile. His top teeth were straight but the

bottom ones were competing for space, smashed together in a slightly crooked row. "And I think those are the only questions you can ask about a name, so do you give up?"

"No, those are not the only questions about a name. Is it a place?"

"I'm sure everyone can find a place with their name."

"So not a place that you know of, then?"

"No."

"Okay, so not Dallas or Houston, then—"

"You have a thing for Texas?"

"Those were just the first ones I thought of." I looked around the car and wondered if there were any clues in there. Mail or notes. There was nothing.

"Are you trying to cheat?"

"Maybe. So your sister's name is Bec. Can you tell me about any special meaning behind that?" I asked, thinking maybe there was a theme.

"That's not a yes-or-no question. Are we done with the game?"

"Okay, Mr. Rule Follower, I withdraw the question."

He turned down the radio that had been the background noise of our conversation. "My sister is named after Rebecca from the Bible, but that won't help you because my dad named my sister and my mom named me. My dad is very religious. My mom's a hippie, free-loving painter."

"Really? How did that happen?"

"My mom entered some paintings into an art show put on by the church my dad attended. Twenty years later and they're still together."

"Cool."

"Yes, they are pretty cool."

I stared at the glowing numbers of the radio station. It wasn't a station I ever listened to, so I didn't recognize the quietly playing song at all. "You know what we've succeeded in doing with this game?"

"What's that?"

"Increasing the anticipation."

He laughed. "I know, right? Can I just be fill-in Bradley forever?"

"No." I turned toward him in my seat. "I really want to know your name."

He gripped the wheel and stared at the road. The sun had set and the sky had turned gray and was darkening more with each passing minute. He licked his lips and his voice went husky and soft. "'The seen, the known, dissolve in iridescence, become illusive flesh of light that was not, was, forever is.'"

I wasn't sure what he had just said but I knew I wanted him to say it again. "That's beautiful. What is it?"

"Part of a poem. When my mom was pregnant with me, she went to see an art show that came through town.

Monet's "Water Lilies" were some of those paintings and a poem by Robert Hayden was displayed with them. She had always loved the painting but that day she fell in love with the poem. So she named me after the poet."

"Robert?"

"No."

"Hayden . . ." I realized I had said it with a bit of reverence and I cleared my throat to pretend that was why.

"Is it disappointing?"

"No, not at all. I like it a lot."

"I'm kind of fond of it as well."

"Way better than fill-in Bradley."

"How is Bradley anyway?" He gave me a sideways glance.

"I don't know. I haven't talked to him since that night." I'd been telling too many lies lately, so I felt the need to add, "He texted me. I tried to call him back and he didn't answer. Then he called me back but I missed it. Then I left a message for him. I haven't decided if I'm going to call him again."

"What's the deciding factor?"

That was a good question. He should've been gone. I didn't need to call him for him to be gone. "I don't know. I shouldn't be deciding at all. He left me at prom. In the parking lot. I wasn't expecting it." I was talking aloud without filtering my thoughts at all, so I shut my mouth before I said other things I didn't mean to.

He raised his eyebrows, but I couldn't read his expression. A large bug hit the windshield with a thump. He turned on the wipers, spraying water to clear it away. "You wanted it to end on your terms?"

"Yes. I mean, no, I didn't want it to end . . . maybe. What about you? Bec was right, wasn't she? You really do want your girlfriend back."

He let out a breath. "Possibly."

That was as close to "of course I do" as it got for guys, I thought, but I played along. "What's the deciding factor?"

He tapped the steering wheel with his thumbs, took a deep breath, and said, "Tonight, I guess."

CHAPTER 13

● ● ● ● ● ● ●

"Hayden."

He laughed as he turned off the engine. "Are you just saying it to say it again or do you actually have something to say this time?"

"Mostly I'm just saying it because I can, but I do have a question."

"What's that?"

"Are you studying acting?"

"Yes."

"Good. You're very talented at it."

He met my eyes. "Thank you."

"And what about poetry? Your mom named you after a poet. Did you come to appreciate it?"

"Are you nervous about getting out of the car?"

"Unlike you, I am not an actor." I was afraid I'd ruin his ploy to get back with Eve due to my terrible acting skills.

"No need to be. We're here as friends, right? No acting involved."

"Right."

He reached for the car door handle.

"Wait! Let me fix your hair."

"Seriously?"

"Seriously. You want her to want you, right?" I thought he'd leave but instead he turned toward me with a tired look on his face. I quickly grabbed the gel from my purse before he changed his mind. "The key is to only use a little." The gel was blue and claimed "Super Support," so I squeezed out a dime-sized drop onto my palm, rubbed my hands together, then pushed them through his hair.

"You actually have really great hair. It just looks like your mom cut it."

"You don't even know my mom."

"Well, any mom." The front of his hair was drooping a bit so I gave it one last pass then smiled. "There."

"Your work is done?" he asked.

I met his eyes and realized my styling process had closed the space between us. I backed up. "Yes, she'll be all over you by the end of the night."

"Who knew hair was that powerful?" He kept his gaze on me, the one that seemed to search my soul, then a smile spread across his lips. My heart gave a jump that surprised me and I quickly dropped my gaze.

I took my cell phone and lip gloss out of my purse and slipped them into my pocket while he opened his door and got out. By the time I'd tucked my purse with the rest of its contents under the seat, he was on my side of the car opening my door. He gave me a hand out. After he shut and locked the doors, he faced the house and I could see him visibly take a breath, the air flowing into his lungs causing his shoulders to rise and fall.

"Are *you* nervous?" I asked, a little surprised.

"Maybe. Thanks for coming with me."

"Of course."

"Okay, here we go."

"Hayden?"

"Yes, Gia?"

"Nothing. I just wanted to say your name."

He smiled, which was what I was hoping for. He just needed to relax. I knew Bec wanted me here to keep him away from Eve, but who was I to stop him if that's what he really wanted? He led me up the walk and around the side of the house to a gate that was propped open.

"Oh. Look at that. Your ex-girlfriend's house backs up to the ocean." I had known we were close to the beach—I could hear the waves and smell the ocean breeze—but I hadn't realized we were this close.

"Pretty cool, right?"

The secluded beach was full of people eating, talking, dancing. Hayden scanned the area and I could tell when he saw her because he went still!. I followed his gaze and went still myself. It wasn't that she was drop-dead gorgeous or anything, but just looking at her, I could tell she had more quirk and personality than I'd ever have. Her hair was a shockingly white blond that she wore choppy, one side longer than the other. Mine was brown and boringly all the same length. She was short and curvy while I was tall and lean. She wore a T-shirt that said something on the front I couldn't read but I was sure it was funny or odd, just like Hayden's were. They belonged together and after tonight they probably would be back together. He wanted it, and from the way she was now looking at Hayden, her eyes lighting up with joy, it was obvious she wanted it too. Bec was going to kill me.

Eve waved and he nodded.

"I'm just going to take off my sandals. I didn't realize we'd be on the sand." Wedges were not right for this. I should've worn flip-flops. No wonder Bec had given me that look.

"Sure."

"Can I just put them back in your car?"

"Of course." He handed me the keys but didn't offer to walk me.

"Okay, then . . . I guess I'll see you in a minute."

I walked back to his car, unbuckled my sandals, and threw them in the backseat. Normally I was so confident walking into a new place. Why did I feel so nervous now? Maybe I shouldn't have come. All I'd wanted was to see Hayden again, find out his motivations for going to prom with me so I could stop obsessing about it. So that things could go back to normal. I'd done that. But I was here now. I could stay for a little while for Hayden's sake. We were only twenty minutes from my house. Maybe once Hayden and Eve got back together, I could call my brother or Claire for a ride and head over to the other party.

I followed the path back to the beach. Hayden had moved about twenty feet farther into the party but was now talking to Eve and another guy. I had several options—a food table across the way, a makeshift dance floor, or a group surrounding a bonfire. Or, of course, I could go see how Hayden was faring. I chose that option.

I took two steps in his direction and my foot landed on something sharp. With a quick breath between my teeth, I checked to make sure it wasn't glass. It was just a piece of a shell and it was only a surface scratch. I brushed off my foot and then joined Hayden.

"So the second I took off my shoes, I stepped on a—"

"Gia," Hayden interrupted, grabbing my hand and pulling me to his side. I stumbled slightly but he held me firm. "I want you to meet Eve and Ryan."

"Hi."

"And, guys, this is my girlfriend, Gia." He slid a hand down my back and gave me a lingering kiss on the cheek after the announcement.

Whoa. What? In the two minutes I'd been gone, something had changed and I wasn't sure what. I turned on a smile and held out my hand. "Nice to meet you."

The guy grabbed my hand. "Good to meet you." When he let go he took Eve's. Oh. And there it was. Bec was wrong. It was option number one Eve was interested in. She wanted Hayden here to make sure he was still pining over her but she was still very much attached to whoever this guy was.

Eve's brilliant smile had faded just a bit as she took me in. From this close I could see her T-shirt. It said, *I like turtles.* I wasn't sure if it was supposed to be funny or if she really did have a thing for turtles.

"You brought someone," she said. "I didn't realize you were . . . dating anyone."

Hayden in all his smoothness said, "I hope that's okay. The invitation said plus one."

The invitation said plus one? And here she looked like she was in shock that he had actually brought someone.

"Right. It did. I know how close you and your sister are so I thought . . . But yes, of course it's fine. Come get something to eat. I'm sure you want to catch up with some people you haven't talked to in a while. Everyone is here."

"Yes, I'd love for Gia to meet everyone. You ready, hon?"

I took his offered hand and squeezed it. "Yes." We started to walk away then I turned back. "Oh, and thanks for inviting us, Eve. This looks amazing. Happy graduation." She nodded me a thanks and then walked the other way.

"I'm sorry, I'm sorry, I'm sorry," Hayden mumbled under his breath as we walked toward a long table full of food by the patio of the house.

"Don't be. I owe you."

We stopped in front of the table and I stared at the food spread before us. "Are you hungry?"

His gaze was on the ocean in the distance, his jaw

tight. It seemed as though he hadn't heard my question at all.

I put my hand on his back. "You okay?" I didn't know why I asked him that; it was obvious he wasn't. He had come here tonight thinking his ex-girlfriend had invited him because she wanted to get back together with him and he had just found out she hadn't.

"Hayden?"

"What? Yes, food. Let's eat. Are you hungry?"

"We can leave. We don't have to stay."

"We're staying." He said it like I had dared him not to and he was rising to the challenge.

"Okay. We're staying. You have other friends here, right?"

He nodded.

"Then let's have fun."

"Deal."

We each filled a plate with food and then found two empty seats at a round table. He greeted several people then scooted his chair extra close to mine. While he ate with one hand, his other was always resting on the back of my chair, or on my shoulder, or playing with the ends of my hair. I knew it was for show and I had to keep telling myself that as chills radiated down my spine every time he touched me.

"Where have you been? I haven't seen you at school lately," a guy from across the table asked.

I was grateful for the distraction because Hayden moved both elbows to the table and leaned forward as he spoke. "I've been around. Busy with graduation stuff."

Busy being a recluse, according to Bec.

"Well, it's good to see you. Where are you going to school next semester?"

"San Luis. You?"

"Me too." The guy looked at me then. "You put up with this guy, huh?"

I smiled.

"You don't go to school with us, do you?"

I started to say no, but Hayden beat me to the answer. "She goes to Bec's new school. We met through her."

In a way, I guess we kind of did. He was dropping Bec off for prom. I dragged him in to be my date.

"Cool," the guy said, then he stood, gave a head nod, and walked away carrying his empty plate.

Hayden pointed at the olives I had picked off my pizza. "What's going on there?"

"I'm not an olive fan."

"There were other options without olives."

"I like the flavor the olives leave on the pizza. I just don't like the texture of the olive itself."

He laughed then popped one of my discarded olives into his mouth. "Weirdo."

"Hey."

"I like weird. Normal is so boring."

"Right." The problem was that I was the very definition of normal. He'd probably just learned the most interesting thing there was to know about me. I was not Eve. Not that it mattered.

I looked around and realized we were the only two sitting at the table now, leaving plenty of room for when Eve and her boyfriend wandered over and joined us.

"I'm so glad you came," she said again when she sat down with her own food in the chair right next to Hayden. So close she could put her hand on his knee when she talked. And she did. It was obvious Hayden had been trying to make her jealous and it was obvious it was working. Maybe he'd get his wish by the end of the night after all.

"I didn't think you would," she continued. Her hand finally came off his leg. I wondered if my death glare had anything to do with it. She had no right to waltz around messing with Hayden's head. He may have wanted her back, but Bec was right. This girl was bad news. I was suddenly on board with Bec's plan of keeping this girl far away from Hayden. I leaned my shoulder against his.

"Why didn't you think I'd come?" Hayden asked,

meeting her stare. I was proud of the way he didn't react, just gave her a look that seemed innocent.

"I should've known you would," she said. "You're such a nice guy. Isn't he a nice guy, Mia?"

"Her name is Gia," Hayden said.

"It's fine, babe," I said to him. Then I looked at her. "I never get mad when people hear my name wrong because I think to myself, Maybe they have hearing issues, excess earwax or something."

Hayden coughed once and I could tell it was to keep himself from laughing. "You might want to get that checked out, Eve."

Eve's expression had gone ten degrees cooler. "I don't have wax in my ears. Sometimes you just mumble, Hayden. Like last year in the school play when the whole audience thought you said, 'I want to kill you,' when you were supposed to say, 'I want to kiss you.'"

Hayden, who had been pretty stoic since we came, cracked a smile. "Well, my line was better anyway."

"I know. Why wouldn't Sky want to kill Sarah, right?" She laughed.

Ryan looked as lost in this conversation as I was. Great—inside jokes.

"Kill me, baby," Eve said in what sounded like a New York accent.

I was willing to kill her if that's what she was asking.

Hayden didn't seem like he was on board with that plan, though, his smile still lingering. Ryan put his arm around Eve and Hayden moved back an inch, his face going hard again. I grabbed his hand and he turned to me. He brushed a kiss to my cheek so I closed my eyes.

When I opened them he said, "I want to dance with you," using that husky voice he sometimes did.

I let him take me to the makeshift dance floor across the sand. I let him wrap my arms up around his neck and then rest his hands on my hips. For one moment I forgot we had an audience and it was for them that we were performing this show. He made me forget I had come here to try to get him out of my head.

He leaned down and I thought he was going to whisper something sweet in my ear when he said, "You're a better actor than you give yourself credit for."

Those words jolted my thoughts back into the right place. "I am, aren't I?"

CHAPTER 14

• • • • • • •

"So, what's the story? Who's Ryan?" I nodded back toward the table where he and Eve still sat, her head on his shoulder.

"He's my best friend . . . well, was my best friend since the fifth grade." A line formed between his eyes with this admission.

"Ouch. I'm sorry."

"It happens."

"That doesn't mean it doesn't suck when it does."

"We exchanged a few black eyes. We're good now."

"Really? You're still friends?"

"No, not at all, but I don't want to beat him senseless every time I see him now, so that's a step forward, I think."

His still-tense jaw made me wonder if that statement was true at all, but I didn't mention this. "I'd say that's a very good step."

He squeezed my hips and then put his forehead to my shoulder. I couldn't help but notice I was a great height for him to do that. He wouldn't have been able to do that comfortably with Eve.

"I'm so sorry," he said. "I told you that we'd come as friends and then I pull this. I guess I just thought . . ."

"That she'd beg for forgiveness tonight?"

"Yes. Is that wrong? I just wanted a little justice. Some karma or something. Instead, I'm playing a stupid game. I don't do this. I don't play head games with people."

I twirled the hair at the nape of his neck, hoping that Eve was watching because his story had made me feel completely justified in playing head games. "Maybe just this once you can give yourself permission to give her a taste of her own medicine. And it's not like I'm unaware of what you're doing. You're not preying on some random, unsuspecting girl to make your ex jealous. I'm fully aware and wholeheartedly in support of making this girl feel at least one small twinge of regret tonight."

"And then tomorrow we'll both be better than this, right?"

I laughed. "Absolutely."

He wrapped his arms around my waist and picked me up, spinning me around once. "You're the best." He put me down and offered me his smoldering stare that he had unveiled at prom. "So, are you ready for this?"

I laughed, not really sure that I was, if he was going to pull out all the stops like that. "Yes."

He took me by the hand and led me in the opposite direction of Eve, toward the beach.

"We're going the wrong way," I said.

"No, this will drive her nuts, seeing us sneak away from the party."

"Oh, right."

"There's a place over here that's a little more private. Hopefully it's not taken." He maneuvered us around some large rocks and then glanced over his shoulder, probably to see if Eve had noticed.

He was right, this was very private. A semicircle of rocks blocked us from the view of the party but gave us the perfect view of the ocean. He'd probably spent a lot of time here with Eve. He plopped down in the smooth sand and pulled on my hand for me to join him. I did. We sat shoulder to shoulder facing the ocean.

"So, you didn't tell me your sister dressed like . . ."

"A drug dealer?"

"That's not what I was going to say. But that's why I didn't recognize her at prom. She looked so different from the way she does at school."

"Yeah, I know. It's just a phase she's going through. She'll be on a new kick in a couple of months."

"What? Why?"

"I'm not sure. I think it might be her way of not letting anyone get too close. She likes to keep the world at an arm's length."

"Has she been burned before too?"

He tilted his head in thought. "No, actually. Maybe she learns well from those around her."

"But you two seem close."

"We are. We have a close family, but maybe that's been a disservice to her because she thinks no one could possibly love the real her as much as we do." He picked up a handful of sand and let it slowly trickle between his fingers. "What about you? Are you close with your family?"

"Yes," I said right away, but then I paused, Drew's words about how my parents hadn't really been there for me after I broke up with Bradley coming into my mind. I shook my head to get rid of the thought and then nodded. "Yes."

Hayden raised his eyebrows. "You sure about that?"

"I'm close with my parents, but my brother—I don't know—he's always trying to stir up trouble. He went away to college, though, so it's generally pretty quiet at home." I thought about how Drew had come home this weekend and offered to help me find out if Bradley was cheating. "But I think he has good intentions. He wants to be a good brother. He just doesn't do it in the best ways sometimes."

"That's good. If he's trying, then he cares."

"You think so?" Maybe I wasn't ready to give up on a relationship with my brother after all. Hearing that he might care more than I thought made me happy.

"Yes, I do." He leaned back on his hands and stared out at the ocean and I watched as several waves crashed on the shore. "I feel like I'm being selfish tonight. I really should get you home."

"It's only, like, eight o'clock."

He lifted one side of his mouth in a half smile. "And shouldn't the little high school student be going to bed soon?"

I laughed. "First of all, there is no school tomorrow. Second, you're in high school too and we graduate in four weeks. Speaking of, why is your girlfriend throwing such an early graduation party?"

"I'm sure everyone is planning their parties for the end of the month and she wanted to be the first and the best.

Plus she's probably going somewhere foreign and exotic the second she graduates."

"Right."

"And she's not my girlfriend." He leaned forward and took off his shoes. "They're full of sand," he explained as he dumped them and set them off to the side.

A print of his hand from where he had been leaning was stamped on the sand between us. I traced a line around it then placed my hand inside of it.

"You have long fingers," he noted, seeing that my fingertips almost reached the top of the print.

"I do. But the bottom part of your palm is missing from this imprint."

"I don't think so." He held up his hand and nodded for mine.

I pressed my hand against his, aligning our palms. The top of my fingers barely reached his first joint.

"I guess you're right," he said. Our hands stayed pressed together for several breaths. "You have sand on your hand." He took me by the wrist and began gently wiping it off.

My phone rang, making me jump. I left it in my pocket.

He let go of my hand. "Don't you want to check that?"

"Not really."

"What if it's your parents?"

I pulled out my phone to see Bradley's name flashing on the screen. Hayden and I stared at it until it stopped ringing.

"Still determining?" he asked after a moment of silence.

I shrugged.

He moved his fingers, gesturing for me to hand him my phone.

"You're not calling him, right?" I gave him my phone.

"Of course not." He opened my text messaging, entered a number and sent off a text. Then he handed me back the phone. I read the message.

I decided that Bradley is no good for me. I don't ever need to talk to him again. He did dump me at prom, after all, and left me alone in the parking lot to find my own way home. Plus he's way too old for me.

"Who did you send this to?"

Right as I asked, his phone chimed. He pulled it out, looked at the screen, then typed in something, and tucked it back into his pocket. He nodded his head toward my phone just as it chimed.

You are so smart. I completely agree. I'm glad you made the right determination. ~H (aka FIB)

I laughed. "You think so, huh?"

"Having been Bradley for a night, I can honestly say

that he is no good for you. I mean, you caught him cheating with that other girl, remember?"

I pushed his shoulder. "I think that might have been his sister."

"Yuck. Even worse."

I smiled. "Well, if you're going to determine things for me, then I get to determine things for you."

"Okay, that's fair. What's the verdict?"

"You know what I'm going to say."

He didn't deny it.

"You deserve so much better. She *really* cheated on you with your best friend. You need to let them both go . . . forever."

As if she sensed we were talking about her, I heard her voice calling out. "Hayden? Are you back here?" And without a second thought, I launched myself at him. I had just meant to jump into his lap, but my momentum sent him onto his back, me landing on top of him.

"Um . . . hi," he said, looking up at me.

"Hi." His eyes were amazing up close—crystal blue.

Eve's voice was louder now, just around the rock, less than three seconds from discovering us.

He reached up and took my face in his hands. He pulled me toward him, the desire in his eyes spelling out his intentions.

"Don't do it unless you mean it," I whispered, inches from his lips. I had meant it as a joke but it came out breathy and serious.

He immediately paused, his eyes changing from desire to worry. He turned my head and kissed my cheek instead. I was both disappointed and relieved all at once. I reminded myself what we were really doing. If this didn't make Eve jealous, nothing would.

CHAPTER 15

• • • • • • •

"Oh," I heard Eve gasp. "Sorry."

We sat up as if caught.

Hayden ran a hand through his hair, brushing off the sand and completely messing up my styling job. "Hi, Eve. Did you need something?"

"No. I mean, yes, um, Spencer is looking for you."

Hayden's eyes lit up. "Spencer is here?"

"He just got here. I told him you were coming."

Hayden jumped to his feet then reached down to help me. He pulled me up so hard that I almost ended up on the ground again. Then he took off, looking back once to make sure I was following. I was trying to, but he was moving fast.

"They have a total bromance," Eve said, and I realized she was keeping pace with me. "Well, I'm sure you already know that."

"I haven't met him."

"No? They're practically the same person. Although Spencer is a little over-the-top to Hayden's go-with-the-flow routine."

I watched Hayden throw his arms around a guy and they patted each other's backs several times before separating. I could hear their laughter from where I had slowed to a crawl about thirty feet away.

"He'd want you to meet him," Eve said, giving me a little push.

"Oh. Right." I really didn't want Hayden to have to extend this lie to people he actually cared about, but with Eve standing right there I felt like I had to. I walked forward until I stood next to Hayden. For the first time I had a clear view of Spencer's face—dark eyes, almost black in this lighting—and I nearly took a step back. I knew him. Well, not really. He went on a date with Laney once two years ago and I had doubled. The only reason I remembered him was because he'd been a total jerk, mean to her the whole date then trying to make out with her when it was over.

Hayden was in the middle of telling Spencer a story about some scene he had to do for drama. " . . . so I asked the teacher, 'Can this be a monologue?'"

Spencer laughed. "What did the girl say?"

"She thought I was kidding."

"And let me guess, you went along with that?"

"What else was I supposed to do?"

"I don't know . . . maybe stop worrying about someone else's feelings for once and worry about your grade."

Hayden shrugged. "Whatever. It turned out fine."

Spencer's eyes drifted to me and I waited for him to recognize me as well but he didn't. He just seemed to be wondering why this strange girl was interrupting their conversation. It had been two years and he hadn't even been my date. It was understandable that he wouldn't recognize me.

Hayden's happy eyes met mine and they seemed to snap back to reality. "Oh, Gia. Hi."

"Do you know this gorgeous girl?" Spencer asked.

"I do. She came with me."

"You lucky dog. How does an average-looking guy like yourself attract a girl way out of your league?"

"I think it must be my killer charm."

Spencer turned to me. "Would you agree with that assessment?"

"He is rather charming."

"Hmm. I thought I had that in droves."

Eve, who had joined us as well, gave a small laugh. "There's a difference between charming and obnoxious, Spencer."

"I'm sure you know that difference well," Spencer said.

Eve raised one eyebrow. I waited for her comeback to him but both she and Spencer laughed. He rushed forward and threw her over his shoulder. "I'll be back. I'm just going to drop this girl in the ocean as part of her graduation present." He headed off like he was going to do that very thing.

"You better not," she said, pounding his back. "Save me, Hayden."

Hayden just shrugged with a big smile on his face.

"Ryan!" Eve screamed.

Both Hayden and I watched as Spencer trudged toward the ocean. Before he made it, Ryan joined them and they had a fake wrestling match in the sand. Hayden let out a sigh. He seemed so happy for the first time tonight. I didn't need to tell him that Spencer had been a jerk to my friend two years ago. Spencer obviously didn't remember and he had probably changed a lot since then. He seemed different, nicer.

"Your friends are fun," I said.

"Yes, we had a lot of fun together."

"You miss it."

"I miss how it was before. Everything is different now and it's pointless trying to make it the same."

I hoped he meant that he had given up trying to win Eve back. Neither she nor Ryan deserved him in their lives.

Hayden was sitting at a table catching up with Spencer when I came back from the bathroom. I approached him from behind and draped my arms over his shoulders, pressing my cheek against his. *Take that, Eve,* I thought as she walked past us with Ryan. The night had cooled considerably and Hayden's cheek was warm. I felt him smile then he laced his fingers with mine.

"You two are sickeningly cute, aren't you?" Spencer said.

Hayden tensed and shifted in his chair. His fingers slipped from mine and he folded his arms over his chest. Oh no. He felt guilty. He wanted to tell his friend this was a lie. I could sense it because I knew the feeling. It had been one thing for me to lie to Jules—I felt like she'd deserved it—it was a completely different story to lie to Claire and Laney.

"Please don't," I whispered in his ear. He couldn't tell him tonight when he had no idea how Spencer would react to this news. For all we knew, he'd run off and tell

Eve and then this night would've been pointless. "You can break up with me tomorrow and let him know."

Hayden offered a stiff nod. I pressed a kiss to the skin right beneath his ear. He smelled so good I wanted to linger there, take advantage of the last few moments of physical contact we'd have. I felt him shiver so I pulled away.

"You ready to go?" he asked.

"Stay and talk for another minute. I'll go grab your shoes."

He looked down at his still-bare feet. "Oh, right. I left them by the rocks. Thanks."

It was getting late. It was darker this time and the path to the rocks a little less clear. I made it around the bend to see two people making out.

"Oh! I'm sorry."

Eve and Ryan straightened up and faced me, Eve flattening her hair.

"Sorry," I said again. "I just needed to get Hayden's shoes. There they are."

I scooped them up.

"Are you leaving?" Eve asked.

"Yes."

"Thanks for coming," Ryan said as I tried to scurry away. "It's good to see Hayden happy again."

It's all an act, you jerk, I wanted to say. *You are the worst friend ever and don't use his happiness to ease your guilt.* Of course I didn't.

"Yeah, sure. See you around."

Hayden was up and heading my way when I emerged from the rocks. "Thanks," he said, pointing to the shoes, when I met up with him. I was so glad I was the one who had found Eve and Ryan behind that rock just then and not him. He didn't need to see it rubbed in his face any more than he already had tonight.

He wrapped me up in a hug and buried his face into my hair. "Thanks for tonight."

I closed my eyes. "Of course. It was fun." And I was surprised to realize that I really meant that. Hayden was easy to be around.

He tightened one arm around my waist and his other hand moved up and down my back. Maybe he wanted to take advantage of the last few moments of physical contact we'd have, as well. "I had fun too. Let's get you home." He let me go and took my hand.

I glanced over my shoulder and sure enough, Eve was standing next to the rocks, staring at us. I should've known his reason for physical contact.

CHAPTER 16

• • • • • • •

We pulled up to his house and he turned off the engine and hopped out of the car before I could stop him. When he got to my door and opened it, I said, "Sorry, I should've mentioned that I need a ride home."

"Oh." He looked up and down the street like he'd see a car waiting for me there. "Did my sister get you?"

"Yes."

"She's so sneaky."

"Yes, she is." I stayed sitting in his car, waiting for him to shut the door and go back around to his side.

He didn't. He nodded toward his house. "Do you need to get home right away? My sister is going to want a report. I bet you'll give a more satisfying one."

The clock on the dash of his car said ten p.m. I had two hours until curfew. "Okay, sure."

We walked the path to the front door and Hayden unlocked it and stepped inside. Bec was sitting on a couch in the living room and she immediately turned off the television and looked between us. "So?"

Hayden put his arm around me. "You'll be happy to know that there were many head games played tonight and much jealousy floating about. I'm not sure exactly who was playing all the games or who was the most jealous, but Gia did all the things that you made her swear to do."

Bec turned to me. "Okay, now I want to know what really happened. None of this vague crap."

At that moment an older woman came sweeping into the room. Her hair was pulled back into a loose bun, held by a pencil. Tons of flyaway strands had escaped the arrangement, leading to a windblown look. "Hayden, I thought I heard you. I need your face."

"Mom, I have a friend over." Hayden pointed at me.

She smiled my way. "I don't see how this affects anything. You can bring her."

Bec stood and followed after her mom, who was already walking down the hall without waiting for a response.

"It's pointless to argue," Hayden said. "She always wins." He led me down the hall and around a corner. Inside a large room with double doors and hardwood floors were tons of paintings. Some finished and hanging, some halfway done, others blank canvases. One rested on an easel, a large sheet covered in paint splatters on the floor beneath it, as if someone had abandoned it right in the middle of painting. We all entered the room.

"This is Gia, by the way, Mom."

"Oh, I'm sorry, where are my manners?" She extended her hand to me. "I'm Olivia. I'm sorry for stealing this boy away but I need his gorgeous face. I mean, tell me that face doesn't inspire creativity."

Both Hayden and Bec rolled their eyes.

"She says that every time she pulls us in here and then she creates things like that." He pointed to a painting of a half-insect, half-zebra face splitting open to reveal a blooming flower. "My face did not inspire that."

"It really did," his mom said.

"She just gets lonely in here," Bec said.

"My children mock me, but they are my muses." She studied me then. "I think you could be my muse as well. Your bone structure is amazing."

"Don't let her fool you," Bec said. "What she means is that she wants to paint bones. Probably dinosaur bones or something while she stares at you."

Olivia did not seem offended by the banter. She just laughed and began to paint while Hayden sat on the stool in front of her. By the way she studied him, it seemed she was using him as a model, but I could see her canvas and it was most definitely not Hayden.

Bec looked at me. "So spill. Tell us everything that happened tonight."

I glanced at their mom, not really sure I wanted to admit to the act of lying in front of her.

"My mom already knows," Bec said. "And while she doesn't condone it, she can see why our immature brains might feel it necessary."

"You are misquoting me, Rebecca. I said that revenge is the product of misdirected emotions but that I had a few emotions regarding Eve as well."

"You did not say 'misdirected,'" Bec said loudly. "I specifically remember you saying 'immature.'"

"Maybe I said 'underdeveloped.'"

"Same thing," both Bec and Hayden said together.

Olivia applied a broad stroke of navy-blue paint to her canvas right beneath the crooked purple eyes already painted there. "My point was that revenge is never the answer."

"Yeah, yeah." Bec waved her hand at her mom then turned to me. "So anyway, tell us about the revenge."

I looked at her mom and wondered if she was upset that they were fighting. She didn't seem bothered at all. "Okay, so Eve was there with Ryan."

"I knew it!" Bec yelled. "They're still together, aren't they?"

I nodded. "But you were right, she wanted Hayden too."

"She did not," Hayden said.

"Then why did she hug you and sit so close and put her hand on your leg?"

"She put her hand on your leg?" Bec's expression went hard.

"She did?" Hayden asked.

"Oh, please," Bec said. "You know she did. Don't try to play all innocent, Hayden. And you probably liked it."

Hayden just met her stare with an even expression that I couldn't read.

"So please tell me you got back at her," Bec said, looking at me.

"There was hand-holding and hugging. We danced."

"And Gia jumped on top of me," Hayden said.

I gasped. His mom turned toward me.

"I did not . . . sort of. It was an accident. I didn't mean to knock you down."

"Tell me she saw," Bec said, smiling.

"She did."

Bec spun in a circle once, her arms outstretched, then she grabbed me by the shoulders and shook me. "You are awesome. Revenge is awesome."

Olivia cleared her throat.

"Because I have a very, very immature brain," Bec added.

"Tomorrow we are all going to be better people," Olivia said, which was almost the same thing Hayden had said earlier. I caught his eye and he nodded once.

Better people. The way they had both said it made me want to try.

CHAPTER 17

. . . .

Hayden slid off the stool.

"Where are you going? I'm not finished being inspired," Olivia said.

Hayden directed Bec onto the stool in his place. "I need to take Gia home. She's had enough of our crazy family for one night, I am sure."

"Bye, Gia," Bec said. "Thanks for doing everything I asked you to."

It's like she said it to remind Hayden . . . or me . . . that tonight was an act, not real. Hayden didn't need to be reminded. He had put on a perfect show.

Olivia gave me a hug without using her hands, which were dotted with paint, pressing her wrists to my shoulders. "Good to meet you. I was serious about that bone structure. Come back and see me."

I smiled.

"Dinosaur bones," Bec said as Hayden and I left.

Hayden glanced at me a few times as we walked down the hall. "My family is weird but I love them."

"Your family is awesome. You're mom isn't . . ." I trailed off, not wanting to bring up a bad subject.

"Isn't what? Normal? Sane?"

I shook my head. "No, of course not. It's just she and Bec were kind of fighting. She's not mad, is she?"

"Mad?"

"About the whole revenge thing."

"No, she's not mad." He opened the front door for me and the cold air bit at my cheeks, making me realize they were hot. "And if you think that was fighting, then you haven't seen Bec fight."

"I just can't believe you told your mom about your revenge plans."

"It's my sister. She's the center of all our craziness."

"I can see that."

"I'm sure you can, considering what she forced you to do tonight."

"She didn't force me," I said. I wouldn't mind hanging

out again, but I couldn't admit that. It felt weird, like I wanted something more from him, and I didn't. We were both putting on an act. It would be completely ridiculous to read into an act.

"Well, I know she asked you to, so thank you. You did really well. Have *you* ever thought about studying acting?"

I laughed as I climbed into his car. "No, I haven't."

"It's fun, though, right? It's like a natural high to perform a scene like we basically did tonight." His eyes were shining and I could see that he'd enjoyed the night for a different reason than I did.

"It was fun."

"My mom's right, though," he said. "It was super immature of me to want payback, but in a small way, I feel a little better now."

"Do you at least have closure? I know that's what you wanted."

"Yes, I do. No looking back."

"No looking back," I repeated.

I directed him to my house and when he stopped at the curb I jumped out before he turned off the engine. I didn't want to make him pretend to be my date anymore. So I was surprised when I was halfway up the sidewalk and he was suddenly beside me.

"You're fast," he said.

"Oh. You don't have to walk me up."

"I can't help it. My dad raised me right."

"Where was your dad tonight?"

"He goes to bed early and wakes up with the sun."

"So your mom named you but are you more like your dad or your mom?"

"Do you mean am I a wild free spirit or a conservative early riser?"

"Yes."

"What do you think?" he asked.

"I don't know. You went to prom with me at the drop of a hat, no questions asked."

"I asked questions."

"Not ones that mattered."

"You were too pretty for those questions."

I smiled and tried not to be too flattered but a few butterflies took flight in my stomach. "Don't you mean too lonely?"

He gave me a smirk. "Well, that too."

We made it to the doorstep and I turned toward him. "So prom night makes me think you're like your mom. But . . ."

"But?"

"But then you walk me up to my door out of the

obligation instilled in you to be a gentleman and that makes me think you're more like your dad."

"My mom might take offense to that."

"Why?"

"Because had she taken you home, she would've probably walked you to your door too."

"So then I'd be standing on my front porch with your mom."

He chuckled. "Yeah, not a great image."

"So you're saying you're like your mom?"

"No. You got it right. I'm a little bit of my mom, a little of my dad, and a lot of me."

"Well, that's a very good mixture." I pulled out my keys to unlock the door. "I had fun tonight."

"What would you have done tonight if you hadn't gone with me?" he asked.

Logan's party. I hadn't even thought about it since the beginning of the night. At first I'd even thought that the second Hayden dropped me off I would head straight there for the end of it, but I didn't feel like doing that at all right now. "My friend from school is having a party tonight. He's thrown some killer . . ."

I trailed off because I couldn't remember the last time a party had really been all that killer. Hayden tilted his head like he was waiting for me to finish. He was giving me that look again, the one where he was searching for something beyond what I was offering. Hadn't he learned by now that what he saw was what he got?

"Go on," he said.

"Never mind. It was stupid."

The front door opened then—how could I forget that my parents always waited up for me?—and my dad appeared.

"Gia?" he said.

"Yes, sorry. I'm coming in."

My dad took one step out. "Hello, I'm Mr. Montgomery."

"Good to meet you, sir. I'm Hayden."

My dad looked at me to explain who this was and I didn't know how. "He just brought me home. Thanks, Hayden."

I walked inside and heard my dad offer a better good-bye than I had then close the door.

My mom sat on the couch reading. "How did studying go?"

"I don't think she was studying," my dad said.

"What?" My mom looked concerned.

"The girl you met earlier? It was her brother. The one I told you about. He gave me a ride home."

"Well, why didn't you say so?" my dad asked.

"I just did." I looked between the two of them, waiting for them to ask more, to accuse me of not being where I said I was. My mom just folded the blanket she'd been using and placed it on the couch. I tried to imagine what would happen if I told them about revenge and fake dating. The images in my brain consisted of a lot of sputtering speeches and confused looks. "I'm going to bed."

"Say good night to your brother too. He's leaving first thing in the morning."

"Okay." I knocked lightly on my brother's door but there was no answer. I cracked it open and saw that he was already in bed.

He rolled over and sat up a little. "Hi, G. You're home."

"Yes. Just saying good night. Have a safe drive tomorrow."

He dropped back onto his pillow. "What was up with Goth Girl earlier? Why are you hanging out with her?"

"She's just a friend. Sort of."

He gave a sharp laugh that caused tension to spring into my chest and I shut his door before he said something rude. Hayden was wrong. My brother didn't want a relationship with me. After spending some time with Hayden and Bec, I could see that what my brother and I had wasn't great.

When I got to my room I started a group text with

Claire and Laney to let them know I wouldn't be joining them. We ended up texting about my date. They gave me the expected responses—lots of exclamation marks and all-caps—which tonight didn't feel as satisfying as they normally did.

CHAPTER 18

• • • • • • •

The morning sun shone through my window and I rolled over, rubbing my eyes. I stared at the ceiling, thinking about the night before, what Hayden and his mom had said about being better. I wondered what a better person consisted of. Where I was supposed to start.

My mom knocked on my door then poked her head into my room. "Good morning. Your friends are here."

"My friends?" My phone said it wasn't even ten a.m.

"Should I tell them to come up?"

"Sure."

She closed my door and I rushed over to the mirror

above my dresser to see how out of control my hair was. It was bad. I had just enough time to run a brush through it before my door opened and Claire, Laney, and Jules burst through, a combination of laughter and perfume.

"Hi." I put a smile on and plopped back on my bed where Claire had sat. "What's going on?" I wondered why they were all together without me. Had I forgotten something we planned?

Claire, who seemed to read my mind, said, "Jules kidnapped Laney and me this morning and then we came over to say hi."

"Oh." I looked at Jules, wondering if that was part of the original plan or if she was hoping to leave me out and then casually mention at school on Monday that they had hung out together.

Jules didn't give away her hand. She just put on a pleasant smile. "I heard you went on a blind date last night? That's crazy. I would never go on a blind date."

"Yeah. Remember, I told you I was going on one when I invited you to come over and help me get ready."

"You never called me. Maybe you thought you did because you called Claire and Laney. You probably just forgot." She smiled sweetly. "It's okay, it's not a big deal."

"Jules. I called you."

Claire looked between the two of us. "Maybe you did forget, Gia."

"You think I'm lying?"

"No, I already assured Jules that you would never lie to us. That's why there must be a different explanation."

I closed my eyes. Right. I'd never lie to them. How could I get upset and accuse Jules of lying to them right now when I was doing the same thing? I swallowed my pride, willing to let this one go, at least until I came clean myself and moved on. "Well, I know I told you, so maybe *you* just forgot."

She shrugged. "Maybe. So was your blind date fun?"

"Yes, it was."

"What did you do?"

Her questions always made her sound like the lead investigator at a crime scene.

"We went to a graduation party for one of his friends."

"So is he weird?"

"No, he's not."

"If his sister has to find dates for him, he must be at least a little weird. I just want to know what favor you owed her to make you agree to dating her brother."

"Yeah, seriously," Claire said. "I'm curious too."

"I just haven't been very nice to her or her friends." Which was true.

"That's good that you could help her out, then," Laney said.

"Yes, it is."

My laptop sat closed on my desk and Jules pointed at it. "Can I use it for a sec?"

"Sure." When she sat down and powered it on, I went to my closet and pulled out clothes.

"Is your brother still in town?" Claire asked.

I narrowed my eyes at her but it was hard to portray anger when I was smiling.

She laughed. "What? Drew and I have a connection."

This time I laughed. "No, he left."

She made an overly dramatic sad face.

"So is this where the kidnapping adventure was meant to end? Or are we going somewhere?"

Laney bit her lip. "Well . . . we're going somewhere, but we knew you probably wouldn't want to come so we just wanted to say hi before we went."

"Where are you going?"

"Matt texted me about ten minutes ago and asked if we all wanted to surf today. I guess his uncle is in town and is this world champion surfer or something and wanted to know if any of his friends wanted some free lessons."

Claire nodded. "We thought we'd make it a group date. So I called Tyler and Jules called Garrett."

I looked at Jules, who was still on the computer. "That sounds fun."

Her eyes swung to mine and she tilted her head.

"It does?" Claire asked. "So you'll come?"

"Why not? I should at least try it before I decide I hate it, right?"

Claire smacked my arm. "That's what I've been saying forever."

"It's about time I listened."

"You should ask your blind date from last night to come with us!"

It would actually be really fun to call Hayden and ask him to go on a group date with my friends and me. I liked hanging out with him. And he'd probably think surfing with some professional was the coolest date ever. But there was a huge problem with this. There were actually probably a lot more problems than just one, but I didn't want to think about how Hayden and I were only acting and he would probably say no to a real date anyway. The main problem was that my friends couldn't see Hayden again, ever. He was Bradley to them.

"It's too soon to ask him out again. But I'd love to come if I wouldn't be some sort of third . . . or seventh wheel."

"Of course you wouldn't be a seventh wheel."

I did feel a little like the odd-numbered wheel, but I could see how Claire might find surfing peaceful—the gentle rocking of the waves as we waited for one to ride, the power of the ocean as it pushed us along. And Matt's uncle was really cool. Without him, I was sure I wouldn't have been able to catch a wave at all on my first time out.

And I'd caught quite a few. But now the others were riding while Claire and I lay on our boards, side by side, hands linked so we wouldn't float away from each other.

"You seem quiet. You okay?"

"I'm good."

"Are you having fun?" she asked.

"Yes, I am actually."

"Don't sound so surprised."

I laughed. "Well, I'm not used to being the worst at something, so that's my only complaint. Well, that and my completely valid original points: the cold water, salt in my hair, and—"

"Sand everywhere. I know." She smiled over at me.

"I'm impressed, Claire. You're really good. And you taught Jules, right?"

She nodded.

"You did a good job. She's good too."

She squeezed my hand. "Should we catch another?"

Just as she asked, Jules paddled up. "Did you see me ride that one? My longest yet."

I sat up on my board and Claire followed. "We missed it." My gaze found Tyler, who was riding a wave now. "Did you see that trick he just did? Way to find a surfer boy, Claire."

"I didn't even know he surfed until after prom."

"And he's Claire's date, Gia," Jules said.

"Um . . . I know."

"It's just you've been flirting with him all day. I thought I should remind you."

"What?"

"Jules," Claire said. "Stop. It's nothing."

I turned my stare to her now because "it's nothing" wasn't even close to "she is not." "I haven't been trying to, Claire, I promise."

"I know, Gia. You're just friendly. Seriously, it's nothing."

Jules gave me a look like, *It's something*, and I wondered if this was something they had talked about before. Me flirting with their guys. I had never flirted, on purpose, with their guys.

"Let's surf," Claire said. "This one's mine." And just like that, she dropped in and caught the wave, leaving Jules and me alone.

"Why'd you do that?" I asked.

"Do what?"

"You know what. Why are you lying about me not inviting you places and now accusing me of flirting with other people's dates?"

"It's time to stop playing innocent and own up to the things you do. You already flirted with Logan when you knew she liked him. Leave Tyler alone."

"I did not flirt with—"

She glanced over her shoulder and caught the next wave.

I was trying not to hate her but she was making it really hard.

As we finished up for the day, paddled into shore on our boards, and said good-bye to Matt's uncle, I saw Bec on the beach with her friends. I cringed. It was the closest beach to where we lived so it wasn't out of the ordinary to see people I knew. I quickly scanned the area to make sure Hayden wasn't with her. He wasn't. That made me relax a little, but I still feared my friends would recognize Bec from prom. I was already on their bad side today with the supposed flirting. I didn't need to add to it.

"Freak alert," Jules said, walking up behind me.

I tried to steer our group in a large arc around Bec and her friends, but the quickest path to our stuff was the one that led right next to them. My attempts to go to the right only resulted in them all outpacing me by staying the course. When I caught up again, I noticed that Garrett, who was carrying both his and Jules's surfboards, had slowed to almost a stop.

"I didn't know they let you all out in the sun," he said. Jules laughed.

Bec met my eyes but then looked back at Garrett. "I didn't know you knew how to speak." I wished she wouldn't egg him on. It only made it worse.

Jules took a step forward, like she was going to walk away, but her foot dragged in the sand and kicked a spray of dirt over the group. They all jumped to their feet, Bec brushing at her face. "Hey!"

"Oops, sorry," Jules said, her tone proving she wasn't.

"Come on, guys," I said. "Leave them alone."

"Yes, listen to your leader," a girl behind Bec said, dripping with sarcasm.

This comment was the wrong one to make. Pointing out my supposed status only made Jules more cruel. She draped her arm around my neck. "Since it's obvious you all have never been to the beach before, our leader would like to share a few rules with you, starting with appropriate beach attire. Right, Gia?"

"No. I wouldn't." I ducked out from under her arm. "You guys can do what you want."

Bec smirked at me. "We didn't realize you owned the beach, but thank you for giving us permission to do what we want."

Jules stared at Bec hard, and just when I thought she was going to throw back another mean comment, she said, "You look familiar."

My heart stopped when Bec's piercing stare met mine

again. She was going to tell. I could see it in the way her dark-colored lips lifted into a smirk. "I go to your school" was all she said.

I took a relieved breath, grabbed Jules by the arm, my rented surfboard still in my other hand, and dragged both the girl and the board away. The others followed. When we'd walked ten steps that way, Jules yanked her arm free.

"Since when do you show charity to the freaks?" Jules asked.

"They weren't doing anything to us. You didn't have to be so mean."

"I wasn't being mean until they told Garrett they thought he didn't know how to speak."

"Garrett started it."

"He was just making a joke."

Why was everyone looking at me like they agreed with Jules? "Whatever. I thought we were going to change and go out."

Claire hooked her arm in mine. "We are. Let's go."

I had just broken up a fight between my group of friends and Bec's group before it got too heated. This kind of felt like being a better person. Too bad my friends weren't on board with my efforts.

CHAPTER 19

• • • • • • •

stared at my computer, confused. The Facebook page of a guy named Bradley was up on my screen. He didn't look familiar and I wasn't sure why this page was pulled up at all. Had my brother been using my computer? I went to close out of the page when my eye caught on a detail beneath his picture—UCLA. My eyes darted to his picture again. It wasn't my Bradley.

Jules.

She'd been on my computer that morning. This is what she looked up. This is what she left up for me to see. But she hadn't discovered anything yet. Was she just trying to let me know that she still suspected something? That she was digging? That she'd figured something out? Why did she care so much? I signed out of her account and into mine. I brought up the real Bradley's page and like I had hoped, his profile was still a picture of a black weight lifter that he admired. Even if Jules found this page, she wouldn't think for a minute it was the right one. I closed out the page then checked my Twitter and email.

The house phone rang and I waited for my parents to answer it before I remembered they were out for a date night. I stood and padded down the hall and into the kitchen just as the answering machine picked it up.

A voice began talking on the machine, leaving a message. "Hi, Mr. and Mrs. Montgomery, this is Professor Hammond at UCLA calling about your son, Drew."

I snatched the phone up, anxiety tightening my chest. "Hello, hello, I'm here."

"Oh, hello. I was just leaving a message."

"Is Drew okay?"

"Okay? Oh yes, of course. I'm one of his teachers and I just wanted to let you and your husband know about an award your son is winning for a short film he made."

"I'm his sister."

"Gia?" he asked.

Drew's teacher knew my name? My heart swelled. I

shouldn't have felt so proud about that but I did. It meant he'd talked about me at least once. "Yes."

"Ah, good to talk to you. Can you let your parents know? And you should come too, of course. He'll be receiving his award and showing a small piece of his film at a banquet this Saturday. Your parents should've gotten an invite in the mail a couple of weeks ago, but I'm calling all the award recipients' families just to make sure they received that. It included four tickets. It's really a special honor. I'm sure he'd appreciate the support."

"That's great. Thank you for calling. I'll let my parents know."

"You're welcome. I'll see you Saturday."

I hung up the phone and went to put it down but changed my mind. I dialed Drew's number.

"Hello."

"Hey, it's me."

"Hi. What's up, G?"

"I just got a call from your professor. Congrats on the award."

It was silent for three breaths. "Oh. Thanks."

"I'm coming to the banquet." I had just made that decision.

"I already talked to Mom and Dad about this. My teacher is making this into a bigger deal than it is. It's not worth the three-hour drive at all. I'd rather you all come to a film festival the school is putting on next month. I have an entry in it that I'd love for you all to see."

"I don't mind coming twice."

"Gia, really. It will be so boring. They're only showing a three-minute clip and between driving here and back and then sitting through a two-hour awards ceremony, your whole day will be wasted."

My happy feelings from before were deflated. "Okay."

He must've heard the disappointment in my voice because he said, "I was just down there."

"But we hardly saw each other."

"I'll make you a deal. Next time I'm down, we'll go out, just the two of us."

I couldn't remember the last time we'd done that. "Okay."

"Good. See you next month." He hung up the phone. He was right. It was probably pointless to go all the way to LA for a three-minute highlight.

My parents came in carrying bags that they set on the counter in the kitchen.

"You're home," my mom said.

"I am. You went to the grocery store for your date night?"

"No, we just stopped by on the way home." She unloaded a gallon of milk. "How was your day?"

"Fun."

My dad tousled my hair. "Did the surfer dude teach you anything good?"

"He taught me never to call him a surfer dude."

My dad laughed.

"Drew's professor called about an award he'll be getting on Saturday."

"That was nice of him to call."

"Are you going?" I asked even though Drew had assured me they weren't.

"We were going to, but Drew told us it wasn't worth it. He wants us to come next month."

"We should go anyway," I said. "Surprise him. He probably just doesn't want to inconvenience us."

My dad pointed to the cupboard above the fridge. "I still have the tickets they sent."

"I scheduled some open houses for Saturday," my mom said, unloading vegetables into the fridge.

"Oh." My eyes drifted to my dad, thinking about suggesting a father/daughter outing, but he shrugged as if he had accepted my mom's excuse.

"We should probably honor Drew's wishes."

"But like I said, maybe he was just saying that to be nice but really wants us to come."

"I don't want to argue about this, Gia," my mom said.

I stopped midbreath. "I wasn't."

"The decision has been made."

"Right." I sighed. "I'm going to go clean my room."

"Thank you," my mom said as I headed out of the kitchen.

But when I got to my room, instead of cleaning it, I sank to the bed. My prom dress still hung over my desk chair, stirring up a longing I didn't like to feel.

On a whim I pulled out my cell phone and sent a text: **I was trying to be a better person today but the world isn't cooperating.**

Hayden texted back almost immediately: Uh-oh. What happened?

I sighed. **I wanted to support my brother, who won an award, but my parents don't want to go. And he doesn't want us to come anyway.**

Instead of the chime of a text I was expecting, my phone started ringing. I jumped then smiled when I saw Hayden's number on the screen.

"Hello."

"What kind of award?" he asked as if we had been talking all along.

"I guess he did some sort of short film. He takes a couple of filmmaking classes."

"You should go anyway," he said.

"That's what I said, but my parents didn't agree. My mom has to work and my dad was quick to use that as an excuse."

"You don't need them."

"Well, that's the thing. I do. I don't have a car. It was like pulling teeth whenever I wanted to borrow it to visit Bradley. And since my mom has to work, that's not happening."

"I can take you."

"Why would you do that?"

"Because I owe you and I'm working on being a better person."

I laughed. "You do not owe me. We're even now. If you did this, I would owe you."

"Bec would probably come too. She loves that artsy film stuff," he said as if I hadn't said anything at all. "It would be fun. An adventure."

I pulled at a loose string on the bottom of my jeans. "I don't know. My brother was pretty insistent about us not coming."

"He probably just didn't want to pressure you. I know that I hate to have people go out of their way for me."

"You're right. He'd probably be happy we came. Maybe he even wanted my parents to insist on coming."

"He probably did. You said you two aren't very close, right?"

"Right."

"This is like you showing him that he's important to you. That you support him."

It felt weird making Hayden drive me three hours,

but he was right, this would be a good show of support. I remembered the conversation I had walked into the middle of between Hayden and Spencer. How Spencer implied that Hayden was too nice, did things without thinking about himself. I hoped this wasn't one of those times. "Are you sure?"

"Of course."

"I'll give you gas money."

"If you want to."

"Thank you, Hayden."

"You're welcome, Gia."

CHAPTER 20

"Don't get any ideas." It was the first thing Bec said to me when I sat down in Government the next morning.

"About what?"

"About you and my brother. He's too good for you."

"I have no ideas." Well . . . maybe I was getting a few ideas, but I was trying not to let them linger. If Hayden was in my life for real, I had a lot of explaining to do to my friends. I had a lot of explaining to do anyway. I needed to come clean. Especially since Jules seemed be unwilling to drop her suspicions.

Bec blinked once, lowering her brow like she'd heard my thoughts, then said, "I'm going with you on Saturday to keep an eye on you. Not because I want to help you or anything."

"I thought maybe we were friends now," I said.

"I'm not friends with anyone who won't acknowledge my existence in public."

"You didn't acknowledge me at the beach either."

She laughed. "Not with the pleading stares you were giving me to keep my mouth shut."

"That's more about prom than anything. They can't know it was you at prom."

"Right. Keep telling yourself that."

It's true, I wanted to insist. If my friends knew it was her that Hayden had fought with at prom, the whole story would've blown up right there on the beach. In front of everyone. I wasn't sure why I needed her to believe this. She really wasn't my friend. I should've been able to brush it off and move on.

But I couldn't. "Hey, I helped you out yesterday. They wouldn't have left you alone."

She let out a single bark of a laugh. "Are you for real? You really thought you did some sort of good deed, didn't you? *Saving us* from the snobs you hang out with. You're practically a saint." With that she turned back around.

★ ★ ★

I couldn't shake off the conversation with Bec all day, so when Claire and I were walking to the parking lot for lunch and I saw her, I said, "Hi, Bec."

She did a double take then just shook her head with a smile. "Touché."

"What was that about?" Claire asked after we passed. "Who was that?"

"That was Bec. She's the one I was telling you about the other day who set me up with her brother."

"Her?" she asked, obviously shocked.

"Yes."

"She's . . ."

"Really cool," I said before she could fill in an adjective I didn't want to hear.

"So are you two friends now?"

"I don't think she wants to be my friend."

Claire grunted. "Don't you have that reversed?"

"No, I don't." My backpack dug into my shoulder so I shifted it to the other one.

"Is everything okay, Gia? You've seemed different lately. Distant."

I took a deep breath and let it out in a rush. "I guess I'm just feeling reflective. We're about to graduate and I'm wondering what I've really accomplished."

"You are one of the most popular girls at school. When people look back ten years from now, they will remember your name. They'll know who you were."

How would other people know who I was when I didn't even know that?

She nodded her head toward where Bec had been. "She won't even enter their minds."

"So, being remembered? Is that what life is about?"

"Better than being forgotten."

"I guess I'd rather be remembered for something, though."

"Like what?"

"I have no idea."

I looked at Bec's retreating back. Maybe a lot of people from high school wouldn't remember Bec in ten years, but the people who did would remember she was loud and confident and sometimes mean but always knew exactly what she wanted.

We reached Claire's car, where Laney and Jules were already waiting.

"Where are we going for lunch today, girls?" Jules asked.

Laney and Claire looked at me like it was my decision. "I don't care. You guys pick."

Claire and Laney exchanged a look like I'd never said that before. I was sure I'd let them pick our lunch spot before. Although now that I thought about it, I remember often declaring I was in the mood for certain things.

I hadn't thought that was a demand. More of a suggestion.

"How about Las Palapas? I feel like Mexican food,"
Jules said.

For some reason, Jules picking made me want to make
a suggestion after all but I didn't. "Sounds good."

When Claire drove, I sat in the passenger seat. When
Jules drove, Laney sat passenger. It's just how it worked,
how we always did it. So when I rounded the car after
Claire had unlocked the doors and I saw Jules walk
straight for the passenger door and open it without
a pause, I stopped in my tracks. Over the hood of the
car, Laney looked at me wide-eyed. I smiled at her and
climbed into the back. Claire gave me one confused look
over her shoulder but then started the car.

"Ninety-six days until UCLA!" Jules screamed out
the window. When had she started in on our count-
down? She rolled up the window, reached forward, and
turned on the radio. Then she started dancing and singing. Claire laughed and shoved her arm.

I sent off a text to Hayden: **I'm having extreme patience with
my frenemy. Does this count as being a better person?**

The same frenemy I met?

Yes.

Being a better person doesn't mean taking abuse.

She's not abusive.

I respectfully disagree.

Is there any other way to disagree?

Many other ways, but I think respectfully is the most appropriate in this instance.

I laughed a little and Laney looked over at me. "Are you texting your blind date boy?"

I smiled and she squealed.

"I don't think I've ever seen you look so happy over a boy before."

That statement wiped the smile from my face. "What? Of course I've looked happy over a boy before."

"I know, but you're . . . I don't know. It's different. You had a shine in your eyes."

Claire teased, "Were you glowing, Gia?"

"What? No. I hardly know him. He just said something funny." I tucked my phone away. Of course I wasn't letting a boy get to me. Especially not Hayden. Our story was way too complicated to turn into something real.

"I don't think you ever told us his name," Claire said.

Because of how hard it was for me to earn his name, I felt a bit protective over it. I wanted to refuse to tell them. But I knew that was stupid. "Hayden."

"Hayden?" Jules said. I wasn't sure if she said it with a

disgusted tone or if she always used a disgusted tone so it was hard to know when she truly was trying to express that emotion.

"Yes. Hayden," I said. "I really like his name."

"Me too," Claire said. She pulled into the parking lot and I was glad to be out of the car. Had there always been this much tension when I hung out with my friends?

I had waited half a week to ask my parents about driving to UCLA with Hayden and Bec but I knew I couldn't put it off any longer. The way my mom had said, "The decision has been made," last time we talked about the ceremony was freezing me up. I rarely fought with my parents. I usually agreed with them. The more I thought of it, the more I realized that I rarely fought with anyone. I didn't like fighting. I disagreed with people in my head a lot but rarely out loud.

But I couldn't avoid it this time. I needed their permission. And the thought of a possible argument with my parents was making my stomach hurt.

We sat at the dinner table eating a Costco rotisserie chicken. This was a bad sign. It meant my mom had worked all day and didn't have time to make food. And when she had worked all day, she was crankier.

"This is really good," I said, picking the chicken off

the bone with a fork, my stomach too tight to actually eat it.

"I'm glad you like it," my mom said.

"How was work?"

"I spent all day with a couple and they still haven't made a decision."

"Buying a house is a big deal," my dad said. My mom leveled him with a look and he added, "But they probably should've researched more online first."

"Yes, they should've."

I waited for my dad to come back with another counterargument defending the couple but he didn't. He kept the peace. Both of them always kept the peace. I opened my mouth and the words, *But it's your job to show people houses*, almost came out. They were so close to coming out that I had to swallow. Now was not the time to say something stupid. I wanted to go somewhere this weekend. I needed their permission.

"So . . . I was thinking and I know you two can't go to Drew's award ceremony but I was hoping I could go."

"By yourself?" my dad asked.

"Remember my friends you met the other night? The girl that I studied with and her brother? They offered to come with me."

My parents looked at each other like they could speak telepathically and were discussing their answer. My mom spoke first. "I thought we'd decided we were going to honor Drew's wishes."

"I think Drew just doesn't want to inconvenience us. And you don't have to go. It would just be me."

"And your friends that we hardly know."

"You can talk to their parents. I think you'd really like their mom. She's very nice." I pulled out my phone. "Let me just text Hayden and get her number."

"Gia, we haven't made up our minds yet."

"I know but this will help you decide one way or the other."

Hey, can I get your mom's phone number?

My mom is already taken but I can see why you'd be interested.

Funny. No, it's for this weekend. My parents need a little persuading.

My mom is really good at that.

He sent the number and I looked up, slowly. It took me a moment to realize I had a goofy smile on my face. I let it fall. "Got the number. Just think about it."

"I don't want to fight about this," my mom said.

"We're not, Mom. We're just talking." I understood Drew in that moment more than I ever had. I'd always thought he was trying to rock the boat when maybe really all he was ever doing was expressing a different opinion. Maybe it was time I started expressing mine.

CHAPTER 21

• • • • • • •

As I waited in the kitchen, looking out the window every minute to see if Hayden had arrived yet, I was happier than I'd been all week. I clutched the tickets to Drew's awards ceremony in my hand.

My mom came in, all dressed up in what I call her realtor clothes, which today was a red jacket paired with a black pencil skirt. "I still don't really feel comfortable with this. I don't know these kids very well and your brother is not even expecting you."

"Mom, it's a surprise. Please don't tell Drew. And you

talked to Hayden's parents. I thought you were okay with this."

"I was. Now I'm feeling uncomfortable again."

"When he gets here, you can meet him. It will help."

She looked at her watch, probably wondering if she had time to meet him. Just when I was about to ask her schedule, the doorbell rang. My mom answered the door with me right behind her. I almost wished Bec would've stayed in the car because the calming effect Hayden might have given my mom, with his boyish hair flopping over his forehead and his disarming smile, was probably reversed by the anxiety Bec seemed to produce in her.

Hayden extended his hand. "Hi. You must be Mrs. Montgomery. I'm Hayden."

"Hi, Hayden."

"Hey, Mrs. M. Good to see you again," Bec said.

"Hi. I just . . ." My mom's brain was going to explode, I knew it. Her politeness was battling with her worry.

"Mom, we'll be fine. Thanks for letting me go. I'll call you as soon as we get there and the minute we get in the car to come home."

She wrung her hands together and Hayden directed his smile to her. This made her release a breath and she nodded.

I hugged her before she could change her mind and

slipped around her and out the door. "Thanks, Mom."

"Be good. Love you."

Bec took shotgun, as if visually showing me where she thought I belonged, and I climbed into the back.

Hayden put the car in reverse. "So your mom doesn't trust us?"

I rolled my eyes. "My mom doesn't trust anyone she doesn't know, but as long as I can get her to mostly agree, I know she won't say no in front of my friends. She doesn't want anyone to think everything is not perfect."

Bec laughed. "I'm glad you know how to manipulate your mom."

"It's more creative guidance."

Hayden pulled out onto the main road. "How was your week?"

"Fine. Yours?"

"Long."

I tried to interpret that one word. "Busy at school?"

"No, the exact opposite. It was just a really slow week. We're gearing up for finals and so it's a lot of review."

"Right. Us too."

"Ugh," Bec said. "You two are boring. Maybe I should've taken the backseat after all." With that she put in some earbuds.

"She has very little of my dad in her," Hayden said.

I laughed.

"Okay, so what are your must-have road trip snacks?" he asked, pulling into the same 7-Eleven that I had followed Bec to the other day.

"I don't know that I have any must-haves."

He opened the door. "Then we better find you some."

"Get me Corn Nuts and Twix," Bec said loudly, not seeming to realize we could hear her just fine. "And get Nate licorice."

Hayden pulled out one of her earbuds. "I'm not your personal shopper and I thought Nate wasn't coming."

His comment produced a long-suffering sigh from her. "He just texted me. He's coming now."

I thought she'd get out of the car and follow us in but she didn't.

"Is she coming inside?" I asked.

"No, she knows I'll feel guilty and get them for her."

I laughed. "She has you conditioned, huh?"

"She really does." He opened the door for me and it announced our arrival into the store with a beep.

"So Nate's coming?"

"Is that okay?"

"Of course. You're the driver. I have four tickets anyway so it works out."

"Oh, that's right. I forgot we had to have tickets for this thing. I'm glad you have enough." He led me to the candy aisle. "Okay, so something sweet is a must."

He grabbed a bag of M&M's. "But it has to be offset by something salty." He picked up a bag of pretzels. "And then, of course, I need some caffeine." He walked to the fridge and pulled out a Mountain Dew. "And that's the perfect road trip combination."

"You go on a lot of road trips?"

"We travel a lot. One summer my mom forced us to take a three-week trip in an RV around the United States. It was sheer torture."

"How so?"

"Did you not hear me? I said three weeks. In an RV."

"It sounds fun to me."

"Says the girl who has never spent three weeks in an RV. It's like living right on top of people. I felt like I was this close to Bec at all times." He took two steps closer to me, pressing his chest against my shoulder. I got a whiff of his body spray and nearly closed my eyes because it smelled so good.

"That doesn't seem so bad to me," I said, looking up at him.

He offered me a smile. "Well, it was." Then he put one arm around my back and grabbed a bag of Cheetos off the rack behind me. He held it between us. "These should be your salty. They're good."

I wrinkled my nose. "Not a Cheetos fan."

He finally took a step back, allowing me to breathe

again. "Okay, what treat *would* inspire you to write a letter to its maker?"

I looked at all the colorful packaging filling the aisle in front of me. Either I hadn't tried enough junk food in my life or I wasn't easily inspired because nothing looked good.

"Nothing?" he asked. "Tough critic. Let's do a visualization exercise. We do this in drama sometimes."

I did visualizations before I gave speeches at school. I'd imagine exactly what I wanted to say and how I was going to say it. I wasn't going to do that in the snack food aisle at 7-Eleven. "It's okay, I'll just get . . ." I reached forward and grabbed the first thing my hand touched.

Hayden raised his brows. "Dried bananas?"

"Yep."

"Fine, what's your sweet item, then?"

"I'm fine with the one item. Besides, it's both sweet and salty."

"You need two."

"Nate gets one," I said, pointing to the licorice Hayden had already grabbed.

"I'm not in charge of Nate."

I raised one eyebrow. "But you're in charge of me?"

"Today I am and I don't think you're grasping the importance of the road trip snack. Close your eyes."

A couple of kids had just entered the aisle with us,

laughing and searching each shelf for something specific.

"Don't worry about them. Close your eyes."

I sighed but closed my eyes.

"Imagine we're driving along and we make a wrong turn and get lost in a dense forest."

"Is there a forest on the way to UCLA?"

"Shhh . . ." He pushed a finger to my lips and I couldn't help but laugh. "We're visualizing, Gia, visualizing."

"Right. Forest," I said sloppily against his finger.

He moved his hand to my shoulder and I wasn't sure if he leaned closer, but his voice seemed both louder and quieter at the same time. "We run out of gas in our attempt to find our way out and get trapped in the forest for three days straight. I, being fearless and strong, decide to leave the car and search out help."

"This sounds like the beginning of every horror movie."

"Another half a day passes and you're famished. You reach for the 7-Eleven bag and pull out . . ."

"If it's been three days, I've probably eaten all my snacks by now."

I could hear the smile in his voice when he said, "There's one thing left."

"Looks like it's your bag of M&M's. You must've been too busy being fearless and strong to remember to take it with you. I'm going to eat those."

He snatched the bag of dried bananas from my hand and I opened my eyes.

"Dried bananas and an extra bag of M&M's it is," he said. "You will not be stealing mine."

"Your game was fun," I called after him as he marched to the register in a pretend huff.

When we arrived at the car, Bec had moved to the back, probably because her boyfriend was now coming.

"Boring people in front." She was all stretched out on the backseat. "Now give me my treats."

"I told you I'm not your personal shopper. I didn't get them."

She didn't say a word, just held her hand, palm up, between the seats.

Hayden shook his head and handed her the items she'd requested. "One day I won't get those."

"One day I'll join the cheer squad and go by Becky."

"Wasn't that last year?" Hayden asked.

"Oh yeah. Guess that wasn't a good comparison, then."

"You were a cheerleader?" I asked, not sure if they were kidding or not.

"She was. A pretty good one too."

I remembered how Hayden had said at the party that she liked to put up a front so that people didn't get too close. I wondered if this was another example of that.

"Pretty good?" She met my eyes. "Don't look so

shocked, Ms. President. I was popular once too."

"Wait," Hayden said. "You're the student body president?"

Bec gasped. "Oh no, were we supposed to bring secret service with us? Is this a security breach?"

Hayden ignored his sister. "I thought you just said you were on the student council."

"I am. President of the student council."

"Is this for scholarship purposes or because you like being in leadership?"

"Both, I hope."

"That's a pretty great accomplishment, Gia. Congrats."

I shrugged, feeling like he was making it a bigger deal than it was. "I guess."

"No, he's right," Bec said, surprising me for the second time today. "There are a lot of people who campaign for that. So you are the most popular of the popular."

"I just happened to be the one on the ballot that the most people knew. I think I only got, like, twenty percent of the vote. The rest was divided between the other two candidates and Mickey Mouse, Elvis, and a hundred other various write-ins."

"So what was your campaign strategy? Did you promise off-campus lunch for all? No PE?"

"I basically spent a lot of time socializing online with

a bunch of people I didn't know to get my name in their heads."

"Smart."

"So let me get this straight," Bec said. "You used people to get what you wanted? Did you unfollow all those people as soon as you won?"

"No. I didn't."

"But you probably stopped talking to them."

Bec had this very special way of making me feel like the worst person on the planet. It was her talent or something.

"Bec, stop being a brat."

I was glad Hayden interrupted because I didn't want to have to explain that now I responded when people engaged but never reached out first.

We pulled into an older neighborhood and up to a run-down house. Bec jumped out of the car and rushed up to the front door. She smoothed her hair before she knocked.

"She has a major crush on this kid."

"I would hope she'd have a crush on her boyfriend."

"He's not her boyfriend. She just wants him to be. Maybe you can help her with that."

"Huh. I could've sworn they were together." I watched Nate come out the door and shut and lock it behind him. The half a foot of space between him and Bec as they headed for the car was way more apparent now. I hadn't noticed it before.

"Hey, Nate," Hayden said as they both climbed into the back.

"Hi," I added.

"Hello."

Doors were shut and Hayden started driving again.

"I got you licorice," Bec said.

Hayden raised his hand. "Well, technically, I got you licorice."

Bec hit him on the back of the head with the package and then handed it to Nate.

"Cool," he said. "Thanks." He tore into the pack right away.

Hayden pointed to the 7-Eleven bag by my feet. "You ready to play copilot?"

"I have no idea what that means."

"It means you get to open my treats for me."

"Do I have to feed them to you as well?"

"Ew. No," Bec said.

Hayden smiled. "I think I can handle that part."

I opened his treats and put them on the center console.

"Now we play road trip games."

Bec groaned. "Hayden, this is why that three-week RV trip was unbearable."

"No, I'm pretty sure that was unbearable because we

had to dispose of our own waste and sleep in bunk beds."

She smiled. "True. But your games came in a close third."

"Yes, my games." He took a pretzel and popped it into his mouth. "So, I Spy or Would You Rather? Those are your game choices. Actually maybe we should play Twenty Questions since Gia here lost so handily the last time she attempted that game."

"Hey."

He laughed.

"You're right. I need redemption. I'm actually very good at that game."

"Prove it," he said.

"I will." I opened my bag of dried bananas. "Okay, think of something."

"You're not actually going to eat those, are you?"

"Why wouldn't I eat these? Now think of something."

He tapped his thumbs on the steering wheel a few times and then he said, "Got it."

I turned back to Nate and Bec. "We'll take turns asking him questions about it, first one to guess wins. If it takes us more than twenty questions, he wins."

"I'm not playing your dumb game."

"Let's play," Nate said.

"Fine," Bec agreed without another argument.

"I'll start," I said. "Is it bigger than a bread box?"

Hayden opened then shut his mouth. "Really? That's your first question? Do people even have bread boxes anymore? Are you eighty years old?"

"I play this game with my parents. That's actually a very smart question. Because if the answer is no, I can automatically rule out a person or a place without having to waste two questions. If the answer is yes, I can rule out insects, rodents, and anything else that might fit in a backpack without having to ask multiple questions."

"That's what you should've asked. Is it bigger than a backpack?"

"Don't critique my questions. I have a strategy."

He bowed his head slightly. "I didn't realize I had played this game with the master last time. Although I should've, with the sheer amount of questions you had about a name."

"So? Is it bigger than a bread box?"

"What size of bread box?"

"I am the asker, you are the answerer."

He smiled. "Yes, it is bigger than a bread box."

Nate went next. "Is it a monkey?"

Bec backhanded him across the chest. "You don't guess until you get more clues."

"I wanted to guess. It's part of my strategy."

"What strategy is that? The dumbest one ever?"

Hayden met my eyes and mouthed, *"See, she needs help."*

I laughed.

"No, it's not a monkey," Hayden said aloud. "Your turn, Bec."

"Is it cold-blooded?" Bec looked at me as she asked this, like she was implying something more with the question.

Hayden seemed to think this as well because he gave her a hard look. "No."

I had a feeling this day might not turn out as fun as I'd hoped.

CHAPTER 22

• • • • • • •

"I don't believe it took you guys three hours to ask sixteen questions. Three hours."

"It was Gia's fault. She took the longest with hers," Bec said.

I laughed. "If you didn't analyze every one of my questions, Hayden, it wouldn't have taken me so long. And we still get four more."

He pulled into the parking lot of the university. "I feel like I need to change my answer to something more exciting after this buildup, like last time."

"Wait. Are you saying your name isn't Hayden?"

He gave me a playful tap on my arm with his fist. "No, I meant that there was a huge buildup last time and I felt like I needed to change my name."

"You can't change your answer. That's cheating. But we will pause the game since we're here."

"Oh, good, more buildup." He parked at a metered parking stall and turned off the car.

I looked out the window at the large buildings looming in front of us. We got out of the car and Hayden locked it.

"I'm excited to surprise him. I've never done anything like this."

He added some quarters to the meter. "I'm sure he'll be very flattered."

"Or irritated. Either way," Bec said with a teasing smile.

Hayden put her into a headlock and she squealed in a way I didn't think her capable of doing. "What's that, Bec? Irritated? What siblings ever irritate each other?" He released her and she punched him on the chest. He stood in between us as we walked, Nate on Bec's other side. After a minute Hayden draped one arm around Bec's shoulder and the other around mine. Oh, good, I'd fallen into the sister category.

I pulled the tickets out to find the name of the building the ceremony was taking place in: Macgowan Hall.

I'd been to this campus a few times, a couple of times for Drew and another couple when visiting Bradley, but I didn't remember where everything was. So we paused in front of a campus map.

My gaze immediately settled on the café where I'd met Bradley. I thought I'd feel something, a tug of loss, a longing, but there was nothing.

"It's probably in the theater and film department, right?" Hayden's finger landed right next to the building I had been looking at.

"You've been here before?"

"No, I haven't, but I'm thinking of transferring here eventually. They have an amazing theater program."

Is that why he wanted to come? To check out the campus, give himself some motivation? "You should just start here, then," I said. It would be so fun to have Hayden at UCLA with me.

"I need to get my generals out of the way somewhere cheaper."

"Yeah, not everyone has a scholarship," Bec said.

How did she know that? Had she researched me or something?

"You have a scholarship to UCLA?" Hayden asked. "I'm learning more about you every minute."

"I need a picture," I announced, partly to change the subject and partly because I had an idea. "The three of you stand there by the campus map."

Hayden started to object but I gave him a little push. "Just do it."

I backed up several steps and held up my phone. "Okay, hmm, Nate step a little closer to Bec. That's better. Actually a little closer. Good, now put your arm around her like Hayden is doing. It will look better." Bec's cheeks went a little pink and Hayden's annoyed look at having to take a picture turned into a smile.

"Say, 'UCLA.'"

After getting something to eat, we arrived at the theater about ten minutes early, but I didn't see my brother anywhere. "Should I call him?"

"It would be fun for him to see you in the audience," Bec said. "Then we can talk to him afterward."

"Okay. Sounds good." It mostly sounded good because I was nervous. He'd asked me not to come and I was worried I was about to ruin his special night by being here. I shook off the feeling. He'd be happy. I knew I would've been if our places were reversed, if I'd seen him in the audience the day I'd given my campaign speech or the many times since that I've had to make presentations in front of the school.

A couple of minutes before six, the lights dimmed and a big screen lit up onstage. I was still trying to locate my brother, who I now thought was sitting in the front row. The back of his head looked an awful lot like the backs of several other people's heads, though: mid-collar-length dark hair. Right as the clock on my phone reached six, a tall man walked out to the podium on the stage and tapped the microphone a few times.

"Hello, friends, family, and, of course, film students. I'm so pleased you could all make it. I'm Dr. Hammond, head of the film department. Welcome to our end-of-the-year awards ceremony highlighting our best pieces of the year. I know your time is valuable so we're going to get straight to it."

My brother was right: this was a fairly slow-moving ceremony. A clip from each film that won an award was shown after the honor it won was announced. The short clips were too short to get into and yet long enough to drag on. I pulled out my phone and texted Hayden.

Can it be used in a sporting competition? It was my turn to ask and I was pretty sure I had narrowed down his answer to Twenty Questions to a few different options. It wasn't a person, it wasn't a place, it didn't breathe, it could be carried.

It took his phone a second to vibrate, and when he pulled it out and read my question, he smiled.

His fingers moved over his screen typing for way longer than it took to write a simple yes or no. I squeezed his knee and he chuckled. Sure enough, when his answer came back, it was an analysis of my question.

Sporting competition is such a general term. Do you mean only a sporting competition? Or do you mean that one of its uses can be in a sporting competition?

Do people like to play games with you? Or is it pretty much a one-time occurrence and then they learn their lesson?

Is that one of your questions? Because that would make eighteen. Also, seeing as how this is the second time you've played this game with me, you tell me.

Bec elbowed me in the side and I looked up to see my brother's name on the big screen with the title of his piece: *Reprogramming a Generation.*

"This next piece," Dr. Hammond said, "is one of my very favorites. The insight and perspective that Drew shows us is raw, honest, and real. And because of those things, along with the documentation process itself, Drew has won the ultimate award this year: overall best piece. Congratulations, Drew. I wish we could see the whole film today because there is so much there, but that's impossible. So let us take a short look at your video and then please come up and accept your award."

On the screen, my brother's name and the title of the piece faded, replaced by the UCLA campus. Students were walking to class, the halls were full, and the camera kept zooming in on people on their phones. Then the scene changed to one I recognized immediately, our house. Drew's voice came on.

"How is selfworth measured today? By the amount of likes a post gets, by how many friends we collect, by how many retweets we accumulate? Do we even know what we really think until we post our thoughts online and let others tell us if they are worthy?" While he was speaking, the camera moved slowly down the hall. My face had gone numb because I knew where he was going. I remembered that camera glued to his face over his last year of visits home.

"G, what are you doing?" he asked.

I was sitting on the couch, my phone out. He asked again. The part he wasn't showing on film was the four times he'd asked me that same question and I answered him. Now he was showing the time where I was ignoring him because he had officially gone past the annoying stage.

"G, what are you doing?"

Finally my on-screen face looked up. "I'm checking our pic that I posted to Instagram."

"How many likes has it gotten?"

My on-screen version smiled then and my real-life self looked down. "Only fifteen. If it doesn't get more, I'm deleting it."

Drew laughed. "Hey, I'm going to make a video of this for my class, okay?"

"Like a Vine or something?"

"No, just for a project."

"This would be the most boring video ever."

The audience laughed.

Bec growled next to me. "I'm having an immature brain again."

"Me too," Hayden said, and squeezed my arm.

"I'm fine," I whispered, trying to make that declaration true.

The film kept going, though, and I wanted it to stop so badly. Now it was just Drew, which was better, walking down the hall again a little later in the day. "If I posted a picture of a tree I'd seen fall in the woods and nobody 'liked' it, would I start to question if it really happened?"

"Real original," Bec muttered.

Now Drew was in the kitchen, where my mom was on the computer probably checking out real estate and my dad was on his phone probably playing a game to relax. Next Drew held his phone in front of the camera, where it showed a text from my mom that said, **Come down for dinner.**

"Did you text me about dinner, Mom?"

She looked up and smiled uncomfortably at his camera. "Yes, it's ready. Go get your sister."

I didn't want him to get me because I knew what

happened next. I was hoping this was a time, like in all the other films we'd seen tonight, that it stopped in the middle of a scene. But I wasn't so lucky. My on-screen self was now in my room.

"Dinner, G," Drew said. This time I was on my laptop. I had been doing homework but he didn't show that part. "How many likes now?"

"Forty likes, five retweets."

"So that must mean it's good."

"Yep." I shut my laptop and stood, smiling at him and the camera. "Your face is likable, I guess. Who knew?"

"Good thing your friends told us that or we'd have never known." I knew he was being sarcastic that day and I was sarcastic right back when I said, "So true." But it only proved the point his film was trying to make. That's when the screen went black. That's when Drew stood up and walked to the podium. He had a confident smile on his face.

"Thank you for this great honor," he said, holding the small plaque that his teacher had handed to him. "And I hope my friends are tweeting this, otherwise it didn't really happen, right?" He pointed to a couple of guys in the front row and the audience laughed. "I too wish more of this film could've been shown tonight because toward the end I show the darker side to this addiction of the need for validation. And a lot of the times the people we crave this validation from are complete strangers. It doesn't matter who is telling us they like something. It's just the amount of people telling us that. So if I get a hundred likes for this later on Instagram, then I'll know it's special." He held up the plaque. "If I get two, it must be worthless. What is this addiction creating? And is it too late to undo the damage?"

I had sunk lower in my chair, not a fan of being the poster child for his mocking take on society. I could feel both Hayden and Bec staring at me, but I was now focused on the red velvet of the seat in front me.

Drew's professor came back on the stage. "Thank you, Drew. And good news—if you want to see this or any of the pieces from tonight in their entirety, please visit this website." The address for a site appeared on the big screen. I didn't want to see Drew's piece in its entirety but I memorized the address anyway.

When the lights in the theater turned on, I jumped.

Hayden put his hand on my shoulder. "What do you want to do? Do you want to talk to him?"

"I want to punch him," Bec said.

"Bec, this isn't about you," Hayden said.

Nate raised his hand. "I want to punch him too."

"He edited it a lot."

"You don't have to explain it, Gia."

This was why Drew didn't want us here and I should've listened.

"I'm fine." I stood up and looked down at Drew, who was surrounded by friends and his professor.

A college-aged girl behind me said, "Hey, that was you in that film. And you had your phone out all through the ceremony. So ironic."

I flinched and Bec snapped her teeth at the girl.

I forced a smile. "I just want to go home," I said to Hayden. "I'll talk to him tomorrow when he's less busy."

"Can *I* talk to him now when he's surrounded by people's opinions that he values?"

Bec gave her brother a shove. "Yes. Do."

"No. I just want to go home," I said again.

After we'd made it through the crowded theater and out onto the campus, I took a deep breath. Hayden, Bec, and Nate were all eerily quiet. I just wanted them to talk and act like everything was normal. If we pretended for now it hadn't happened, this would be a whole lot easier.

When we got to the car, I settled into my seat. My first thought was to pull out my phone and distract myself from the reality of what had just happened, but I couldn't do that right now, not with the image of me doing that very thing still playing over and over in my mind.

Hayden started the car and drove out of the parking lot. "If it's any consolation, I don't think he was singling you out. He was just using you as an example to illustrate his point. He was saying it's a generational problem, not specifically your problem."

I nodded.

Bec punched his arm. "That's not a consolation. That was her brother. He shouldn't have done that. Period."

"I know," Hayden agreed.

"That's not the problem anyway," I said in a voice I wasn't sure they could hear.

"What is?"

"The problem is that it's true. I am that person." I did care what other people thought about me. I did delete pictures or tweets that didn't get enough likes. I did measure my worth in those terms. I was possibly the most shallow person on earth and I was just now discovering it.

"We're all that person, Gia. That's why he won the award. It was relatable."

Maybe Hayden was right, but for whatever reason I felt like it applied to me the most. I leaned my head against the window and let my eyes drift closed.

CHAPTER 23

When I opened my eyes, the car was still. Bright over-head lights made me squint and blink a few times. I sat up and stretched.

Bec cleared her throat. "You're awake."

"Where is Hayden?"

She pointed out the window where Hayden and Nate stood at a gas pump.

"Oh. Gas." I reached to the floor, picked up my purse, and dug for my wallet. Pulling out a couple of twenties, I stuck them in the cup holder in the center console.

Bec stared at them for a moment then said, "I'm going

to tell you something and I'm mostly telling you because I feel sorry for you after what happened tonight but I'm also telling you because it's true."

"Okay," I said, wary. That didn't seem like the kind of lead-in that would result in something I wanted to hear.

"You said that the reason you were so upset is because you are that person, the one your brother was railing against in his stupid film."

"Yes."

"And it's true. You were that person."

"Thanks, Bec."

"I said 'were.' You aren't anymore."

I understood what she was trying to say, how she was trying to cheer me up, but I knew better. I was no less shallow today than I was when my brother filmed me six months ago.

She must've sensed I didn't believe her because she went on. "You seem to be trying harder lately. You said hi to me at school in front of your friends. You helped my brother out with Eve. And we've been together for eight hours now and I don't want to strangle you. That's got to mean something."

I gave a short laugh. Her list of my supposed good deeds was painfully short.

Hayden got in the driver's seat and his eyes found mine. "You okay?"

"I'm fine." That was the third time I'd said it and the third time it wasn't true. I pointed to the cup holder. "Thanks."

He looked at the cash sitting there. "What's that for?"

I made myself smile. "A good time."

Nate snorted a laugh and Hayden smiled but it looked forced as well.

My phone rang and I gasped, remembering I'd forgotten to call my mom when I got in the car like I promised. I answered immediately. "Sorry, Mom, I'm on my way home. We're, like, an hour away."

"I was worried."

"I know, I'm sorry. I forgot to call."

"Well, I thought maybe you went out to celebrate with your brother afterward, so when I couldn't get a hold of you, I called him."

"You did?" I squeaked. "What did he say?"

"He didn't answer so I left a voice mail. He must've been busy."

"Yes. I'm sure he's out with friends or something. . . . What did you say in the voice mail?"

"I just asked if you were with him because you hadn't checked in even though you promised you would."

"I'm sorry," I said again, but all I could think about was that my brother now knew I had been there. I wondered how long before he listened to that message and what he'd say when he called me. "I'll see you in a little bit."

"Okay. Drive safe."

"Thanks, Mom." I hung up.

Bec said, "He knows?"

I checked my phone to make sure I didn't have any missed calls from him. "Not yet. But he will."

An hour later, after dropping off Nate, we pulled up to Hayden's house and I met his eyes once again, confused as to why he wasn't taking me home.

"Out," he said to Bec.

"Fine. Whatever."

I got out too and pulled her into a hug before she could go in the house. "Thank you for coming today and for trying to make me feel better."

She squeezed me once. "I said I didn't want to strangle you. That doesn't mean I want to hug you." I could hear the smile in her voice when she said it. "Thanks for helping me with Nate," she said right before she was gone.

Hayden had stepped out of the car too and he gestured for me to follow him. He led me to a swing on the porch. "Sit," he told me.

"You still think you're in charge of me?"

"I don't like the words 'I'm fine.' My mom tells me those two words are the most-frequently-told lie in the English language. And I don't need her to tell me that. There is no way you are fine after what happened tonight."

"Hayden, I appreciate what you did for me today. So much. But I really can't talk about this right now."

The look he gave me then made my heart ache. He felt sorry for me . . . again. "I'm worried about you. And I can't send you home like this because you've told me how little you talk to your parents and I know the kind of people your friends are. And now I've seen your stellar brother. This is going to eat you alive. I just want you to talk it out. Let it out."

"That's not how I deal with things." For a small space of time I'd thought I understood my brother. I thought I'd discovered this great mystery about why he fought with my parents—that he was just trying to express his opinions. But if this was how expressing opinions made the other person feel, I was perfectly fine with going back to the strategy of keeping the peace. Keeping everything inside.

Hayden sat on the porch swing and it was obvious he wasn't moving until I said something. I wasn't sure what was left to say. Nobody had ever tried so hard to get me to open up before. Maybe if I just started talking about other things, he'd realize I didn't want to dwell on this. If I did, I wouldn't be able to contain my emotions. I sat down next to him. "We've never had a porch swing. Do you sit out here a lot?"

"Not as much as you'd think a person with a porch swing should."

"I don't know that I've ever analyzed how much a person with a porch swing should use it."

"Well, I have and it's underused."

I smiled. "Is it a surfboard?"

He paused for a moment as if confused then nodded. "Yes."

"Seventeen questions."

"That was eighteen."

"No, because you didn't answer the sport competition one. You just analyzed it."

"True."

I brought my knees up onto the swing with me. "Do you like to surf?"

"I do."

"I was just surfing the other day."

"I know. Bec said she saw you out there."

Bec had told him she saw me out there. I wondered if she told him how badly my friends had treated her. How badly *I* had treated her. I had been so proud of myself that day over nothing. I had done nothing for her, only for myself. I wondered if Hayden was starting to add up all the negatives he was collecting on me.

He didn't seem to be thinking about the injustices delivered to Bec when he said, "That's what made me think of a surfboard for the game. Very anticlimactic, I know."

He looked at my mouth, and just when I thought he was thinking about other things, better things, things that were going to make me forget tonight completely, he lowered his eyebrows with a frustrated sigh.

"What?"

"You're smiling."

"That's a good thing, right?"

"Gia." He paused and took my hand. "It's not how you're feeling."

"I don't cry, if that's what you're waiting for."

"What are you thinking about?"

"I was thinking about surfing. Now I'm thinking about the fact that your hand is warm." And that I really like holding it.

"That's it. You're talking to my mom."

"What?"

He didn't answer me, just stood up and went inside. He couldn't have been serious. I was not talking to his mom. And yet a couple of minutes later, Olivia came outside and joined me on the porch swing.

I spoke first. "I'm so sorry. Your son is overreacting. I really just want to go home."

"Okay, let me drive you."

"Thank you."

It's like Hayden knew that his mom was the easiest person in the world to open up to because after I told her where I lived and before we had even made it down the block I was rambling on about how that video made me feel. "I'm the most shallow person on the face of the earth, I've decided. I have absolutely no depth. And I don't know how to get it. My life is normal. My parents are together. They don't beat me or anything. Death has never taken anyone close from me. I do well in school. We're not poor but we're not rich either. I've never had a life-threatening illness or injury. I'm devoid of tragedy and therefore have no wisdom or insights to offer."

Olivia laughed. Not the mocking kind of laugh but just a warm, gentle laugh that lightened my mood a bit. "Oh, Gia, honey. You'll have enough trials to get through in life without wishing them upon yourself."

"But I'm flawed. I'm flawed because I haven't experienced anything to teach me any valuable life lessons that make me a better person. My brother captured that so well and easily."

Olivia was quiet and I was convinced it was because I was a lost cause. She had no advice to offer the naive, shallow girl. But then she gave a small hum and said, "We rarely find depth by looking inside of ourselves for it. Depth is found in what we can learn from the people and things around us. Everyone, everything, has a story, Gia. When you learn those stories, you learn experiences that fill you up, that expand your understanding. You add layers to your soul."

I nodded even though she was driving and probably couldn't see me. She pulled up in front of my house and turned toward me.

"What your brother did? It wasn't right. He should've asked your permission."

"He kind of did. On the video itself."

"You and I both know he should've asked in a better way. Mocking someone else to make us seem deep or intelligent only proves the exact opposite."

"He knew it would bother me. It's not like he thought I'd be fine with it. Otherwise he would've wanted me to come."

"I'm sorry, Gia. And I know you're embarrassed. I hope you'll talk to your parents about it. Tell them how it made you feel. Let them bring your family together over this."

I gave a humorless laugh. "We're not like your family. We keep everything on the surface. Or completely inside."

"Well, maybe you're the one who's going to change that with your newfound depth."

I smiled. "Maybe." I reached for the door handle.

"And Gia?"

"Yes?"

"My son doesn't like shallow girls, so there must be a lot more to you than you think."

"Hayden doesn't like me. We've just had a mutually beneficial arrangement that is now, unfortunately, over." He had felt like he owed me a favor after the party. But now that favor was paid. We were even. And I realized after spending the day with him that I was sad about that. I wanted him to like me because as much as I'd tried, I could no longer deny the fact that I liked him.

I gave her a half smile and climbed out of the car. "Thank you so much for the ride."

CHAPTER 24

My parents greeted me when I walked in the house.

"How was it?" my dad asked, his face hopeful. I wanted to do exactly what Mrs. Reynolds suggested and tell my parents everything. But I wanted to give Drew a chance to explain first. Because I didn't want to hurt my parents and hoped beyond anything that maybe I had just seen the worst part of the video, that maybe I'd go online and see that really his piece wasn't mocking his entire family in one fell swoop.

"It was okay. Can we talk about it tomorrow? All that driving made me tired."

"Of course. I'm so happy you got to be there for your brother," my mom said. "I'm regretting now that we didn't go."

"No. It was probably better that you didn't. He was busy." I paused while staring at my mom. "You're still wearing your makeup."

The subject change seemed to throw her for a moment. She brought her hand to her cheek. "Yes, of course."

"It's late."

"I haven't gotten ready for bed yet."

"Sorry to make you wait up." On my way to my room my phone chimed. I pulled it out.

Don't watch the video. It isn't pretty.

Hayden's text didn't stop me. I had to watch it. I had to know what was up on the internet for the entire world to see. I changed into my pajamas and grabbed my laptop. I tried to watch the piece as if it weren't me on the screen. As if it were some other seventeen-year-old girl. Even though I couldn't do it completely, even for the small moment I tried to visualize it, I was still humiliated for the girl with the social media addiction. The girl addicted to the validation of strangers. She didn't even know what she thought until someone told her what to think. She didn't even know who she was. It killed me to know that Hayden had watched this.

I shut the laptop a little too hard then buried my head under my pillow. Hayden was right. I shouldn't have watched that. I should've left well enough alone with the three minutes I'd already seen.

Drew called around nine a.m. I didn't want to answer the phone but I wanted to hear his excuse. I wanted him to have one.

"Hello."

"Gia, you weren't supposed to come."

I didn't speak. I didn't think I could. If that was his excuse, it wasn't a very good one.

His tone became defensive as he rushed on. "I told you right there on the video that I was going to use it for a school project."

Tears pricked my eyes. I forced them down like I always did. "It's just . . . I thought you wanted to talk to me because you cared about me not because you were doing some project."

"Gia, of course I care about you. I'm trying to help you and a lot of other people by bringing this out in the open. Did you know that it's actually been proven that Facebook can cause depression? Comparing yourself to others, the need for validation, it's not good for our mental health."

"Well, your film managed to do that better than Facebook ever has for me, Drew. It made me feel like crap. Like some shallow, idiotic girl who doesn't even know her own mind." It took a lot to admit that to him. It was hard enough admitting it to Hayden's mom.

"That was the message I wanted the audience to get. They were supposed to see themselves in you."

"I don't think it worked. I was made fun of after the ceremony."

"Then those people were idiots."

"That didn't sound like an apology."

"I should've told you about it."

That still didn't sound like an apology. "When did you turn into a pretentious jerk?"

"I posted it on Facebook. Didn't you notice?"

I let out a small gasp.

"Gia, I—"

I hung up the phone then because it was that or yell obscenities at him and my head already hurt enough.

I ripped a piece of paper out of the notebook sitting on my desk and wrote down the website where his video could be found. Then I marched into the kitchen, my chest so tight with anger that I thought I might pass out. My parents were sitting at the table, my dad reading the Sunday paper, my mom the real estate section. They both looked up when I slammed the piece of paper onto the table.

"Whoa," my dad said, a smile coming to his lips. "What's that all about?"

"Your son is a douche. Just thought you should know. Dad, I'm borrowing your car. I'll be at the library." With that, I marched out of the kitchen.

My parents were shocked into silence behind me.

The librarian lowered her brow disapprovingly. "I don't think we have any biographies on people who had to deal with d-bags."

"What about pretentious jerks? Who do you think is the biggest pretentious jerk in history? I want to read his biography." Mrs. Reynolds had told me to learn people's stories. I thought this was a great start and maybe it would help me deal with the one in my life.

The librarian's face lit with understanding. "Did you just go through a breakup? I do have books on how to deal with that."

"No, I didn't. I just want to read a biography. What is the most popular biography?"

"Presidents are pretty popular as well as Einstein, Anne Frank, Cleopatra."

"Cleopatra? Was she that Egyptian queen or something?"

"Yes, the last pharaoh of Egypt. She was a powerful

woman who was ruthless a lot of times. Even refused to share power with her own brother."

"Yes. That. Where?"

"Let me show you."

I was forty pages in when I got a text from Hayden.

You okay?

Did you know that Cleopatra had to marry her own brother?! Marry him!

Um . . .

It was customary. But gross, right? She hated him. Mainly because she didn't want to share power with him. I'm sure he didn't make a "documentary" starring her, though, so really, I don't know what her beef was. I'm sure I'll find out soon.

Did you just use the word "beef" in a sentence?

Do you have a problem with that?

I might. Where are you?

I'm finding depth.

Are you okay?

I showed my parents the video.

What did they say?

I don't know. I'll find out soon enough.

I feared seeing my parents' reactions. I was already mad enough at my brother. I wasn't sure I could handle more anger when faced with their hurt too. Especially because it wasn't often I saw them hurt. They were so good at playing The Perfect Parents that I wasn't sure how The Devastated Parents would look. My phone vibrated with an incoming call and I answered it with a whisper.

"Hello?"

"Why are you whispering?"

I closed the book, left it on the table, and walked toward the door. "I'm in the library."

"That's where all the Cleopatra facts were coming from?"

I opened the door and stepped outside. A breeze lifted the hair off my forehead and I sat on the closest bench. "Yes. What are you doing?"

"Not much. I called because you weren't answering my text."

I was confused. "I answered your text, like, five times. Did you send me another one?"

"You avoided my question, like, five times. I was asking if you are okay."

"Oh. Yes. I guess. I don't know."

He laughed. "Is this multiple choice?"

"My brother's just a jerk, you know."

"Oh, I know. I'm sorry, Gia, I really am."

"You know what's funny? He couldn't even say sorry about what he did, and it was *his* mistake and you had nothing to do with it and I think you've apologized three times." On a whim I added, "Are you busy?"

"Just practicing a scene."

"Do you want to get ice cream? I'll run lines with you."

He hummed a little and I thought he was going to turn me down so I added, "My friends and I always get ice cream when something bad happens. It's how I get over things." I cringed, angry that I chose to make him feel sorry for me again to get him to meet me.

"Okay, sure. Text me the address."

CHAPTER 25

• • • • • • •

It wasn't until after I hung up the phone and texted him the address that I realized I was not dressed appropriately for a date. Not that this was a date. But it was definitely an I-have-a-crush-on-this-guy-and-want-him-to-actually-like-me-and-not-continue-to-feel-sorry-for-me-so-I-shouldn't-show-up-in-yoga-pants-and-a-tank-with-no-makeup kind of thing. It was too late, though. He'd have to see me this way unless I wanted to cancel.

I didn't want to cancel. It didn't matter anyway. He had seen my brother's home video of me and I had looked—well, aside from dumb and shallow—awful.

And maybe worrying about him seeing me look awful on top of dumb and shallow made me even more dumb and shallow, but it's how I felt. And I really wanted to see him so I pushed those thoughts aside. I'd had a bad day and the idea of seeing him was the only highlight so far.

It was cold in the ice cream shop. I wondered if they had to keep it cold for the ice cream or if it was the workers' preference. Because as the eater of the ice cream, I wanted a little warmth. I always ended up at the metal tables outside.

I looked at all the flavors again while I waited for Hayden, not sure if I should order without him or wait.

"Are you ready?" the guy behind the counter asked.

"I'm still waiting for someone," I told him again.

"You go to my school," he said. "Gia, right?"

My eyes snapped to his. Another person I didn't know. Being in leadership lent itself to people knowing my name and me not knowing theirs in return, but I was feeling extra sensitive about that fact lately. "Have we met before?"

"No."

"Good," I said with a sigh, then realized how it sounded. "I mean, not that I wouldn't want to meet you, I just thought I forgot your name."

He pointed to his nametag, which said, *Blake.*

"Oh. Right. I just meant that I thought I should've known your name without having to look and . . . never mind."

"Are you ready to order yet?"

I raised my eyebrows. Was I picking up that habit from Hayden?

"Oh yeah, you're waiting for someone." Why did he say that like he didn't believe me? I hadn't been waiting too long, had I? I glanced at my cell phone. I'd been here for fifteen minutes. Maybe Hayden wasn't coming after all.

"I'll just wait outside . . . is what I would've said a few days ago."

A line of confusion formed between his brows.

"So . . ." My eyes went to his nametag again. "Blake. Are you a senior?"

"Yes."

I nodded. "What's your story?"

"What?"

"I mean, what do you like to do? Are you into sports?"

"I run track."

"Cool."

The door opened accompanied by a beeping noise and I turned toward it with a relieved breath.

Hayden greeted me with his easy smile. He had on glasses that I had almost forgotten he wore. He looked cute in them. How had I ever thought guys wearing glasses weren't my type? I had a feeling anything Hayden wore at this point would become my type. "Hey."

He didn't even take in my outfit like I thought he would. He just walked to my side and peered in at the flavors along with me.

"What's good?" he asked Blake.

"I don't know. I'm not really an ice cream fan."

"What?" Hayden asked, his voice incredulous. "How does a guy who doesn't like ice cream end up working in an ice cream shop?"

"My parents own it."

"That makes sense. How long have they owned it?"

"Twenty years."

"So you grew up here?"

Blake pointed to the floor. "I basically grew up right here."

"Raised by ice cream. I can understand why you might not like it."

Blake laughed. "I loathe it."

And that's how you find out someone's story, I thought. How did he do that so naturally?

Hayden smiled over at me. "What are you getting?"

"Um . . . I was looking at the Rocky Road but I'm not a huge fan of nuts."

"Blake, Gia here likes the flavor of nuts but not the

texture. Can you pick them all out for her?"

I elbowed him in the side. "Actually I don't like the flavor either."

"Then why would you even consider Rocky Road?"

I shrugged. "I don't know. I like the other things in it so much that they almost outweigh the nuts."

"Gia, you are weird."

"Thank you. So what are you getting?"

"I was thinking about vanilla but then I thought, 'That is so boring. Gia will think I'm the most boring person ever.'"

"It's true."

"So then I thought, 'I bet Blake here will tell me what to order,' but he was no help whatsoever. Thanks a lot, Blake."

"No problem."

"So now I'm thinking strawberry is my only option." He nodded his head once to Blake. "This size." He pointed to the middle cup then turned to me. "You're still looking at the Rocky Road. Why are you still looking at the Rocky Road?"

"I don't know. It looks so good and then I talk myself into thinking I'm going to like it this time and I never do."

"I will save you from yourself, then. You cannot get the Rocky Road. Anything else . . . except vanilla because that's so boring. Who would even think of getting that? I don't even know why they stock it."

I smiled.

"It's actually the most popular ice cream flavor," Blake said while adding a scoop of strawberry to a cup.

"Well, I feel validated now. I should've gotten the vanilla."

My shoulders tightened with his word choice. Validation. The thing I was apparently unhealthily addicted to. Maybe I should ask Twitter what ice cream flavor I should eat. "I'll have the Caramelo crunch," I said before I started feeling too sorry for myself. "Same size."

We each paid for our own ice cream and I led him out of the cold to a black metal table outside. He sat down then immediately stood back up, pulling something from his back pocket and dropping it to the table—a booklet that had been folded in half and was now slowly unfurling.

"You said you'd practice lines with me. I wasn't kidding about needing to. I perform this tomorrow."

"Oh, of course." I grabbed the play, but my eyes lingered on him.

"What?" he said. "You're looking at my hair like you want to whip out your little bottle of gel and fix it for the third time."

I smiled. I hadn't been thinking that at all. His hair

was him and it was growing on me. "No, I like your hair and your glasses too, by the way. You look cute."

He pushed them up on his nose. "My eyes were tired after all that driving yesterday."

"Sorry."

"No, please. I wanted to."

I nodded and read the title of the play. "*The Odd Couple*. Is this that one where the one guy is a mess and the other is a neat freak?"

"Yes, it is."

"And you are?"

"A mess." Then he looked at the book in my hands. "Oh, you mean in the play? I'm the neat freak. Felix."

"So wait, you're a mess in real life?"

"Yes, can't you tell?"

"You seem put together."

"Oh, I'm tidy enough. I'm just a mess."

"How so?"

"In more ways than we have time to discuss." He pointed to the book. "Act two, scene one."

"Well, if you're a mess then I'm a natural disaster."

"The cutest natural disaster I've ever seen."

My cheeks went warm. "Okay, act two, scene one."

CHAPTER 26

● ● ● ● ● ● ●

We'd run through the scene twice and I'd only had to prompt him once. "You make a really good slightly crazy guy."

He bowed his head. "Thank you."

"So who plays Oscar?"

"Just another guy in my class."

"Is he as good as you?"

He met my eyes with a smile. "How am I supposed to answer that? If I say no, I sound conceited. If I say yes, you'll think I'm nothing special."

I stirred my spoon around my empty cup. "I wish I could go watch the scene."

"You'd be bored."

"No, I wouldn't."

"Do you like to watch live theater?"

"I don't know. I've never been."

"Really?"

"Really."

Hayden put his hand over his heart. "I'm shocked, Gia. I don't know if we can be friends."

Just as I was about to laugh, I heard a voice from behind me that stopped me cold.

"Gia?"

I closed my eyes for a beat then turned around to see Jules. "Hi."

Jules smiled at Hayden. "Bradley, right?"

I cringed, took a deep breath, then said, "N—"

Hayden stood, and cut me off with, "Yes. And you are?"

Hayden knew who Jules was. It wasn't apparent from the look of innocence on his face, though. I wanted to laugh but I managed to keep it in.

"Jules. We met at prom. . . . You probably don't remember because you were busy with . . . things." She looked between the two of us. "I didn't realize you two were back together. Gia was just telling us about this other guy she was dating."

"No, I'm not dating that other guy," I said quickly, worried Hayden would think I was telling people we were dating. I pointed to Hayden. "And we're not dating either. We're just talking." Was she trying to get me in trouble with "Bradley" by telling him I was dating someone else?

She looked me up and down. "Did you just come from the gym? You're looking very . . . natural today."

"You're right," Hayden said. "She's a natural beauty." Hayden had transitioned into his Bradley role well. He even reached down and took my hand in his, regardless of the fact that I'd just told Jules we weren't dating. I shot him a look but didn't take my hand back.

Jules zeroed in on the script sitting on the table. "Whose script? I thought Gia said you take business classes."

"I take a drama class as well. It's an outlet for me."

"How fun." She adjusted her purse strap on her shoulder. "You wear glasses," she said to him, almost like she was compiling a list.

"When I'm not wearing contacts, yes."

"Gia never mentioned you wore glasses."

I could feel my forehead wrinkle. "Why would I?"

"That just seems like something you would mention.

Well, anyway, I'm picking up some things for my mom. You know how she is. Call me, Gia."

We didn't call each other. She moved up the street. Hayden stood there next to my chair, my hand still clutched in his, staring after her.

"I'm not a fan of that girl."

I squeezed his hand then let it go. I would've hung on to it for as long as he'd let me but his eyes were gleaming in that way they did after he had put on an exceptionally good show. I didn't want to just be part of a role he played anymore.

He sat back down, picked up his script, and folded it in half. "Does she remember everything you ever say?"

"Only so she can use it against me in the future."

"Why do you hang out with her, again?"

"Because my other friends like her."

He stared down the street, where she was no longer visible. "Did I make it worse?"

"I don't think it can get any worse. It's fine." I stirred my spoon around my empty ice cream cup again then bit my lip. "I was going to tell her, though."

"I know, but I think you should tell your other friends first."

"You're right. I need to tell my other friends first." I'd been trying to deny that fact. I'd been trying to pretend like I didn't need to tell them at all. That we'd all moved on. But it didn't work that way. I'd been keeping a secret from them and that's not what friends did. I needed to tell them the truth.

A couple of minutes later I saw Jules emerge from the coffee shop up the street holding a cup. "I'll be right back." Claire's words echoed through my mind. *Just try to be nice to her. She's been through a lot.* I had told Claire I would. I hadn't been trying at all.

"Jules!"

She stopped and turned. "Yeah?"

"I just . . ." I had no idea where to start with her. I thought back to the things she talked about when we were together with the group. She had an awful relationship with her mom. I had originally thought she was just complaining about her parents like we all did, but it was obviously worse than I realized. "Is everything okay? With your mom?"

"Did Claire tell you something?" She sounded angry.

"No. Last time we were all at lunch you mentioned you were fighting. Are you guys still fighting?"

She stared at the Styrofoam cup in her hand. "We're always fighting."

"About what?"

"She wants to move . . . again. I just want her to wait until I graduate, until I'm gone to college, but she's running from man number fifty-one or seventy-five. I've lost count. She already has half the house packed."

Wow. That sounded awful. I couldn't imagine my mom picking up and moving every time there was trouble. I felt bad. "I'm sorry." I remembered her saying something about how much her mom dated. Usually horrible men.

Her eyes snapped up to mine and hardened. "It's no big deal. Claire said I could move in with her for a few weeks if that happened."

"Oh. Well, good. That will help. I just wanted to see if you were okay."

Her gaze went over my shoulder to where I'd left Hayden sitting. "Are you pretending to care because you're worried about me or worried about what I know?"

"What?"

She smirked. "Watch your back, Gia, I'm getting warmer." She started to walk away then over her shoulder said, "Ninety days."

CHAPTER 27

• • • • • • •

Jules had killed the mood, and seeing as how I had avoided home for four hours now, I knew I had to face my parents. So I told Hayden I'd better go home and we parted ways. I wondered if my parents had already called and talked to Drew. I wondered if I was going to walk into a pit of hysteria when I arrived home. I couldn't even picture it.

I braced myself and walked through the door. It was quiet. I wasn't sure if that was a good sign or a bad one. I made my way through the entry and headed to the living room, where I could hear a television or something. *Oh, please tell me they aren't watching it right now*, I thought. But when I got to where they were both sitting on the couch, my mom in her realtor clothes, my dad holding a plate of lunch, I saw they were both watching television.

My dad laughed at something that was said.

I cleared my throat. "Hi. I'm home."

My mom picked up the remote sitting next to her and turned off the television. "Gia, you can't go running off like that again, okay? There is a proper way to ask for permission to go to the library and it wasn't that."

"Okay . . ." I looked between the two of them.

"You've been behaving very differently since you started hanging out with that Bec girl."

"What? I hardly hang out with her at all."

"Well, I can't help but notice that your new contentious attitude has coincided with her arrival in your life. I'd like you to have some space from her for a while." Contentious attitude? Those were always the words she used on Drew.

"This has nothing to do with her. Did you watch Drew's video?"

"Yes, we did," my dad said.

"And?"

"And it was an interesting piece on the changing culture and the side effects that can come from it." He set his plate on the coffee table and moved to the edge of the couch cushion.

"He used our family as his example."

"Who else's family was he supposed to use? He only has the one."

"I don't know, a family who wanted to be part of a documentary where they would be mocked."

"It wasn't mocking. It was just a take on society."

"Maybe you feel that way because you weren't in most of it. I was. I felt mocked."

My mom placed her hand on my dad's arm then spoke. "Oh, Gia, I'm sorry you feel that way. I can see how you might, but I hope, once you're separated from it for a while, you can see it wasn't intended to mock you."

"Well, after the whole audience was laughing at me last night, it's going to be hard to feel like that wasn't the intent."

"It's a piece on society, Gia. Try to take it for what it is."

"So you're going to let him get away with this? You aren't even going to talk to him?"

"We already did. We told him that we wished he would've been more clear when he was home about what exactly he'd be doing with the filmed pieces and that he hadn't been very thoughtful of your feelings but that it was a very well-done piece. We're proud of him."

I swallowed hard. "Proud of him?"

"Aren't you?"

"No. I'm not. I'm mad at him."

My dad nodded. "I understand. I hope the two of you can work through that."

My mouth dropped open and a hot surge of anger burst in my chest and stung behind my eyes. Words that I wanted to say sat at the back of my throat. If I said them, it would only make my mom think I was being contentious.

I cleared my throat, hoping to sound calm when I asked, "Can I go to my friend's house?"

"Which friend?"

"Claire."

"Of course. Don't be back late and call if you go anywhere else."

"Okay." I left the house, feeling suffocated, like I couldn't breathe. I started to drive to Claire's but changed directions at the corner and headed for Bec's house instead. Maybe it was because I was mad at my parents and needed to do something slightly rebellious in that moment or maybe it was because I really wanted to see her. Either way, that's where I ended up.

It wasn't until I was standing on her porch, knocking on her door, that I worried she might not want to see me.

Mrs. Reynolds answered the door. "Gia. So happy to see you."

"Is Bec here?"

"She is. Let me go get her. Please come in."

I stepped right inside the door and pulled it closed behind me. After a few minutes Bec came down the hall dressed in sweats and a T-shirt. Her face was free of makeup and she looked so different. Younger? Less angry?

"Gia. What are you doing here?"

"I'm angry."

"Okay . . ."

"I need someone to let me be angry."

She gave me a little smile. "Well, that's my specialty. Come on." She led me back to her room and pointed at the desk chair. "Sit. Start your rant whenever you're ready. I will be here to egg you on." She plopped down on her bed then she stood up again. "Hold on. I feel like we need some angry music as our background." She pulled out her phone, scrolled through a few screens, then pushed Play. Music poured through some wireless speakers on the bookshelf. She adjusted the volume so it wasn't too loud.

I laughed.

"Laughing and anger do not go together."

"Stop trying to make me laugh, then."

"I'm not. I'm totally with you on this. What are we angry about again?"

"My brother."

She raised her fist in the air. "Totally with you. Carry on."

"So he called this morning, not to apologize but to tell me I wasn't supposed to be at the stupid ceremony."

"He did not."

"He did."

"That jerk."

"And then my parents watched the video."

"Were they crushed?"

"No, they were proud."

"Proud?"

"Yes!" I stood and started pacing the room. "They told me they hoped I would be proud too, eventually."

"They watched it? Are you sure?"

"I didn't see them, but I'm pretty sure."

"That's lame."

"It is, right? Am I being stupid? Do I have the right to be mad?"

"Gia, I'm mad and I'm not even you."

"But you're mad about everything."

"Not entirely true, but I do enjoy my angry times." She sat there for a moment, on her bed, staring at me. "Well?"

"Well, what?"

"You're angry. What are you going to do?"

I stopped pacing, my shoulders still tight with tension. "I don't know." I'd obviously felt angry before but my goal had always been to smash it down, keep it inside, not let anyone see it. I groaned when I realized that I was just like my parents. That's what they always did. They didn't like us to express bad feelings because that would imply our family was less than perfect. Even my mom's appearance always portrayed perfection. They kept everything inside. I kept everything inside.

"Scream."

I looked toward the door. "I'm not really a screamer." Even realizing what I just had about my parents, about myself, it was hard to just let go of that, to let go of a lifetime habit. But I wanted to. I needed to. My insides were on fire and I knew I needed to let some of those feelings out.

"Just scream."

I took a deep breath and screamed.

She smiled. "You have a lot of work to do but that was a good start. Now let's scream at your brother."

"I'm not calling my brother."

"No, I just mean scream things and hope he can hear them. Like . . ." She threw back her shoulders. "What's his name again?"

"Drew."

"Drew, you are a huge jerk and a horrible brother!"

"Who doesn't even know how to apologize right!"

"And who has funny-looking hair!"

I tilted my head. "You think his hair is funny looking?"

"For sure. He needs to cut it shorter or grow it out longer. You can tell him I said that."

I laughed.

"It helps a little, right?"

"Yes." It really did. The fire in my chest wasn't quite as red hot.

She lay back on her bed and looked at the ceiling. I looked up as well and saw that, along with the nature photographs on her wall, she had some on the ceiling too. "Those are great pictures. Do you collect them from all the places you visit?"

"I take them."

"They're yours? I didn't know you were a photographer."

"I try. We went on this three-week trip around the States. That's where I took most of them."

"Hayden told me about that trip."

She smiled. "That's right. I'm sure he said it was like a trip to the underworld or something, and I like to pretend that too, but we both loved it. He forced us to play his stupid games. We fought a lot and laughed a lot and learned a lot."

"I think it sounds fun."

"'Fun' probably isn't the right word, but it was an experience."

In the quiet that followed her statement, I felt awkward, like I hadn't earned the right to be here asking for her help. We hardly knew each other. "So . . . are you doing anything today? Hanging out with Nate?"

She sighed. "No. It's hard to just hang out with him. Nate is just . . ." She shrugged. "I don't know. He's just Nate."

"Do you want him to be your boyfriend?"

"Sometimes." She picked up her pillow and flipped it over then patted it a few times. "And sometimes I want to strangle him. I think I might need to get the second impulse under control before I work on the first."

"Why do you want to strangle him?"

"Because he's clueless. He has a crush on this other girl who is totally out of his league."

My head snapped up. The accusations Jules had made of how big a flirt I was, the angry look Bec had given me when I first met her, all came to my mind.

Bec caught my eye. "Oh, please. Not you."

"I didn't think it was me."

She rolled her eyes. "You totally thought it was you."

My cheeks went hot from the accusation.

"Whatever. You were right to think it because you do represent the type of girl he likes. It's why I hated you at first. Well, that and you crushed his band."

"That was *his* band?"

"He's the drummer."

I sat back in her desk chair. "Maybe you should scream that."

"That I hate you?"

"No, that Nate is clueless."

"Nate, you're clueless!"

"You have the most awesome girl standing right in front of you and you're busy being blind!" I screamed.

"So blind!"

The door creaked open and Hayden poked his head in. "Should I be worried about what's going on in here?"

CHAPTER 28

• • • • • • •

Hayden hadn't seen me yet but my cheeks still went red. His eyes were on his sister, a small smirk on his mouth like he really wasn't surprised at all the screaming coming from her room.

"We're exorcising our demons," Bec said, looking at me.

That's when Hayden's gaze drifted to me and his eyes went wide. "Gia. What are you doing here?"

"I just told you," Bec said. "We're expelling evil from our bodies."

"Wait, you were screaming too?" he asked as if he didn't believe that.

"Yes, she was," Bec answered for me. "Now leave us be. We might need to scream about you next. Do we need to scream about him?"

"No, we don't," I said.

"Too bad. I had some good ones," Bec said.

Hayden crossed his arms. "I'm so confused."

"Her brother's a jerk. Her parents are proud of that fact. We're screaming about it. What's so hard to understand about that?"

"Your parents weren't upset?" he asked me.

"Not even a little bit."

"Ouch. I'm sorry."

I shrugged one shoulder. "It's not a big deal."

Bec sighed. "Gia, it is a big deal. We're angry about it. That's why we're screaming. Aren't you mad at your parents for denying their feelings? Stop doing what they've taught you so well."

Hayden smiled. "You came to the right place. We don't hide feelings around here. There's a bucket of baseballs in the backyard if you're interested."

Bec sat up. "Ooh, yes. Let's take them to Will's place."

"Will's place?" I asked.

Hayden looked at his phone, probably checking the time.

"You don't have to take us anywhere," I said. "If you're busy."

"He's not busy. Let's go," Bec said.

"I am, actually," he said. "But seriously, it helps. You two should go." He gave me a small wave and left the room, disappointment taking his place.

"What's he busy with?" I asked, trying to sound casual.

The look Bec gave me proved I'd failed. "Who knows? Maybe he's going out with his friends or something. He does have a couple of those."

"Right." I ran my finger along the rim of the jar that held her sea glass. "Do you know if he's talked to Eve since the party? Or did our efforts pay off?"

"Are you worried about that?"

"No . . . I mean, yes. I met her and you were right—she's not good for him. But I know his going to her party with me really did make her jealous. I guess I'm worried it did the opposite of what you were intending."

"You think she broke up with Ryan to pursue Hayden again after seeing the two of you together?"

"I don't know."

"Hmm." She scrunched her lips to the side. "Then we better make sure he won't want her back. Tomorrow after school. You, me, and Hayden throwing baseballs at Will's place."

I shook my head. "Bec, I'm done scheming."

"Scheming? This isn't scheming. It's just spending

time with my brother. Where's the harm in that?"

Spending time with her brother. I could feel the tug in my heart at the thought and knew that any more time spent with her brother might lead to a lot of harm on my side. I was starting to like him. Too much. And I usually didn't let myself do that with so little assurance that the feeling was mutual. But I found myself saying, "Okay."

We had driven a good twenty minutes and had reached a country neighborhood where every house looked in need of a face-lift. Hayden pulled up a long dirt drive. The property was lined with large trees and even more junk. Rusted-out old cars, broken appliances, large pieces of farm equipment.

Dogs, several of them, ran up to the car as we drove, barking and chasing us.

"Where are we? This looks like the setting for a mass murder."

Hayden smiled at me. "This is Will's house. He's a member of our church, and for twenty bucks, he lets us throw baseballs in his yard."

"Couldn't we have thrown baseballs in your yard for free?"

"Yes, but he lets us throw baseballs at his stuff." Bec pointed to an old car we were passing with a large hole in its windshield. "It's very satisfying."

Hayden honked the horn and an old man came out of the dilapidated house and called to the dogs. They all barreled toward him. He locked them behind a gate and then went back in the house with a grumpy face that seemed to say he really didn't want us here.

"He's in a good mood today," Bec said.

"That was his good mood?"

"Normally he makes us lock up the dogs and it's not as easy as he made it look."

"If he doesn't like you coming here, why does he let you?"

Hayden turned off the car and grabbed the bucket of baseballs from the backseat. "He loves us."

"He loves our money," Bec said, holding up a twenty. "I'll go pay him."

"That was the saddest attempt to throw a baseball that I've ever seen," Hayden said after my . . . sad attempt to throw a baseball. It didn't even shake the windshield let alone put a crack in it.

"Just picture your brother's face behind that wind-shield," Bec said, tossing a ball and catching it over and over.

"Imagine him holding up his video camera," Hayden added.

"Do you guys keep this bucket of baseballs just to use over here?" I asked.

"No, we have it because Hayden tried to play once in high school like all his friends. But not *all* the baseballs in *all* the world could make him athletic."

"Thanks, Bec."

"What? It's true."

"You didn't make the team?"

"My heart wasn't into it."

"He's been friends with the same group since elementary school. They all got athletic. He got . . ."

"Don't say it," he said to her.

"Geeky."

"She said it."

I laughed.

"He felt left out and lonely. That's why he tried out for the team. Not because he liked it."

Lonely. Hayden felt lonely with his group of friends. Was that why he thought I was when he first met me? He seemed to sense what I was thinking because he squeezed my arm and said, "I'm not lonely. Now, throw the ball."

I got ready to throw again and he said, "Okay, come here. You need direction." He pulled me closer then positioned himself behind me.

Bec groaned. "Are you really using the 'let me help

you learn something' move?"

I couldn't see Hayden's face so I wasn't sure if he was blushing as much as I was.

"This isn't a move, Bec. She really needs help."

"Hey." I elbowed him in the stomach and he laughed.

"If I wanted to make a move, I'd do something like this." He put his hands on my waist, pulled me back against his chest, then leaned in close to my ear. "Hey, baby, you need help learning how to throw a baseball?" He said it in his low, husky voice.

I froze, the entire back of my neck and right ear tingling to life. Bec must've seen my face because she started laughing. Hard.

He stepped back. "What? Was that not very good?"

"Oh no, I think that would've worked if you were trying to pick up Gia," Bec said through her laugh.

"Whatever. It wasn't that good," I said.

"Okay, so now the real lesson." His hands were on my waist again positioning me. "You want to angle your body slightly. Then you'll step with this foot and then throw. Use the step to add energy to the throw." He backed away completely now and I was tempted to tell him I didn't quite understand so he would show me again.

"I don't know if I should be taking advice from

someone who didn't make the baseball team."

"Throw the ball," he said in an even voice.

I smiled and threw the ball.

"Better."

"Except you need to scream something at it while you throw." Bec picked up a baseball and yelled, "Wake up and see what you're missing!" as she threw the ball.

Hayden raised his eyebrows. "Who was that directed at?"

"Stupid boys."

"Got it." He passed me another ball.

"Don't forget to yell," Bec said.

It was more embarrassing with Hayden here but I tried anyway. "How hard is it to ask?" The ball bounced off the windshield.

Hayden twisted a ball between his palms. "Would you have said yes if he asked your permission to use the footage?"

"I'm not sure. Probably not."

He nodded.

"Hayden?" Bec said, pointing at the ball. "Have any demons to exorcise?"

Hayden stared at the windshield for a long moment. Several balls littered the tall yellow grass around the rusted car. Unlike Bec and I, Hayden didn't yell anything angry, but the speed at which his ball hit the glass made me think that maybe he did have a few demons. The glass let out a loud pop and several spiderweb cracks formed from the point of impact all the way across the windshield.

It was my turn to raise my eyebrows at him. "What was that about?"

"It's fun to break things" was his answer but I wasn't sure it was the real one.

We all threw several more, and after a few minutes, Hayden held up his hands. "Okay, stop."

"Why?" I asked.

"It's going to shatter," Bec said.

Hayden grabbed a ball out of the bucket and tossed it in the air. When he caught it he held it out to me with a wicked little smile. "It's all you."

I took the ball from his hand. "If I don't break it, I'm going to be really embarrassed."

"You'll break it."

I angled my body slightly, stepped, then threw. The windshield shattered with a satisfying crack. I smiled. "That was awesome!"

"So cathartic, right?" Bec asked.

"Yes." I let out a happy sigh.

Bec picked up a few balls from the ground. "I'll go play fetch with the dogs for a little bit. Be right back."

Hayden started picking up the balls, throwing them back into the bucket. I helped him. "You guys do this a lot?"

"Not really." The amount of broken or cracked windows on the surrounding cars seemed to say the opposite.

"Did he recently bring that car in?" I asked, pointing to an equally rusty but completely free-of-damage car that sat by a tree across the yard.

"No. We don't touch that one. It's a '68 Camaro. I've been trying to convince Will to sell it to me since we started coming here, but as you saw, he's kind of a grumpy old man set in his ways."

"But I thought Bec said he liked money."

"She was kidding. I think what he really likes is visitors. Come on, you should see this car."

CHAPTER 29

• • • • • • •

Hayden headed toward the car and I followed. "This car is pretty far gone. It would take a lot to restore it anyway."

One side window was rolled down and the interior was filled with dried leaves, the seats were ripped, their rusty springs visible. It didn't stop Hayden from grabbing hold of the roof and swinging himself in, feetfirst, through the window. He rested his wrist on top of the steering wheel and put on a model-like expression: squinty eyes, slightly parted lips. "What do you think?"

I laughed. "It looks good on you."

"I agree. Care to join me?"

The passenger seat seemed even dirtier than the one he sat on. He must've seen my hesitation because he reached out and grabbed for me. I jumped back with a squeal. He dropped his hand, patting the outside of the door like it was a beloved pet. I surprised myself by walking forward, and climbing in through the window, headfirst, right over the top of him. He let out a laugh and helped me through. It was a tight squeeze with him sitting in my way, and my hips brushed against his chest and the steering wheel. My pants snagged on something and I was jerked to a halt, my hands on the passenger seat, my feet still out the window.

"I'm stuck," I said.

"Yeah, you are." His voice contained a smile.

"Help me."

He laughed. "But I'm kind of enjoying this."

"If I weren't using my hands, I'd beat you right now." I tried to pull my leg forward again and was greeted with a ripping sound.

Hayden laughed but then I felt him reaching for my ankle, where it seemed the problem was. "It's stuck on the lock. Let me try to unhook it."

My arms were starting to shake from holding myself up.

"Got it," Hayden said, and tugged my leg free, sending

me jolting forward and face-planting into the seat.

"Ouch."

"Oh no. I'm so sorry."

My legs were draped across his lap, my arms stuck beneath me. The stick shift had bruised my side for sure. I carefully rolled to my right, toward the seat, and he helped me sit up.

"You okay?" He took in my face.

"I'm fine." I rubbed my hands over my face, sure it was covered in dirt. He picked a leaf out of my hair. "I'm good," I assured him with an embarrassed laugh.

"That was really graceful."

I hit his arm and he pretended it hurt.

"Well, I hope this was worth all that," he said, a smile on his face.

I glanced around at the dirty interior that looked even worse up close. "Yeah, not really," I said with my own smirk.

He leaned back against his seat then reached over and took my hand in his. Okay, so maybe it was worth it.

"How did your *Odd Couple* scene go today in class?"

"Really good. Thanks for your help yesterday."

"You didn't need my help."

"I need your help." The way he said it made it sound like we were no longer talking about practicing lines for a play.

Maybe he wasn't. "What demons were you working out today?" I nodded my head toward the car we had battered.

"Ones that should already be worked out," he said vaguely.

I wondered if he was referring to Eve, but there was no way I was going to bring up her name just in case he wasn't. Not when he was holding my hand of his own free will and not because we were pretending for anyone.

"Do you ever wonder if who you pick as friends says something about who you are?"

So he wasn't referring to Eve. He was referring to Ryan, who had betrayed him with her. Or maybe he was referring to the fact that he was lonely in his group, an outsider. I thought about his question, thought about my friends and what that might say about me. I even thought about how Bec's friend had accused me of being mean because of something Jules had said. "Are you talking about Ryan?"

"I'm talking about a lot of things, but yes, he was my friend."

"It was his choice. You can't control what he does. His choice says nothing about you."

"But doesn't it? He was willing to turn his back on a lifelong friendship for a girl. Shouldn't I have seen that coming?"

"You couldn't have predicted that. It doesn't mean you'd do the same thing just because you chose him as your friend."

"I know. I just feel like I should be over it already."

I squeezed his hand. "He hurt you. That's not easy to get over."

He sighed.

"What Bec said, about you being different from your friends . . ."

"I'm not lonely," he answered almost too quickly.

"But you don't really relate to them like you want to?"

"I like sports and sometimes they come to plays. It works out."

"But you feel left out?"

I waited for him to tell me that Bec was wrong again but instead he said, "So did the baseball-throwing experiment help? How are you feeling?"

"I had a fun day, and considering everything that happened the last few days, I think that's a good thing. Thank you for making me laugh."

He studied my face and I smiled to reassure him. He said, "I don't want to be thanked for that. You don't seem to have a problem laughing. You're good at putting on that face. It's what's behind the smile that I wonder about. You don't have to be perfect all the time."

I rolled my eyes. "I'm not, believe me."

He brushed at something on my face, probably some dirt from the seat. "I like it when you're not perfect."

I felt my cheeks get hot again and this time I couldn't hide it.

"What about you, Gia? Do you ever feel lonely in your group of friends?"

I found myself automatically wanting to say no. But he was right. I did always put on a happy face. This whole day was supposed to be about letting go. Letting my feelings out. It wasn't something that came easily to me but Hayden made me want to try. "I never used to."

"But now?"

"I don't know. I love my friends, but yes, I'm discovering that they don't know me very well. It's not their fault, though. I've never let them. I've never really known myself."

"Isn't that part of being a teenager? Discovering who we are? Who we want to be?"

"I hope so because otherwise I'm really far behind."

"I think you know yourself better than you think."

From across the yard Bec yelled out, "Where are you guys?"

Hayden backed up and I realized how close we had gotten. "Guess we'd better get going."

It took me several deep breaths to even out my breathing. Hayden climbed out the window and then turned back toward me.

"Can't I use the door?" I asked, scooting over to the open window.

"It's rusted shut." He reached out his hands. "I won't let you fall this time. Promise." His eyes twinkled as if remembering my not-so-graceful entry.

I moved to my knees, trying to avoid the exposed springs, and put my head and shoulders out the window. I used the doorframe to push myself up and twisted so I was now sitting on the frame, my upper body facing the car, my legs still inside. That's when Hayden scooped me up, putting one arm beneath my legs and the other around my back, and lifted me out of the car. I let out a surprised yelp and threw my arms around his neck for support.

Even when I had cleared the window he held on to me for several breaths. Finally I looked up, wondering why he wasn't putting me down.

He met my eyes. "I had fun today too."

"Good," I said, more breathy than I intended.

Bec appeared behind him. "Did you use the 'climb over me into the car' move on her? I swear, you're pulling out all the stops today."

My previously fast-beating heart seemed to drop, and

as if to emphasize the feeling, he put me down.

"It wasn't a move, Bec," he said, steadying me while I took a few wobbly steps.

She shrugged. "I'm pretty sure you don't have to put on the moves to ask her to the play on Friday."

Hayden narrowed his eyes at her.

She offered him an innocent smile. "I'm going to get the baseballs. Meet you at the car."

And then Hayden and I were alone again. He ran a hand through his hair. "She's really subtle, yes?"

"You don't have to," I said at the same exact time he said, "Would you want to?"

"I know," he said at the same time as I said, "Sure."

We both laughed. "Okay, let's try talking one at a time," he said. "You first."

"I was saying, don't feel like you have to ask me just because your sister told you to."

"I don't. In fact, I was going to tell you that you had to go to the play because I can't be friends with someone who's never seen a live play before."

"Well, in that case . . ."

He looked to where Bec was throwing balls into the bucket. "I don't know how you won her over, but you have."

"Just ten minutes of screaming out our problems seemed to work."

He smiled. "She wouldn't have let you in her bedroom in the first place if she didn't like you."

"I don't think I earned it in any way." I wondered if she really liked me or if I was just the lesser of two evils in her mind. "But I like her."

"So, Friday? Six."

"Sounds good."

CHAPTER 30

. . . .

I sat at the head of the table, the other members of the student council staring at me, waiting for me to say something. I usually enjoyed leading discussions, but so far I had been useless in this meeting.

"Gia," Daniel, the vice president, said, "I think we're ready to move on to item number two."

"Right." I looked down at the paper in front of me. Item number two was one I had fought for, an all-night graduation party on the beach. "Did everyone complete their assignments?"

"We're good on permits," Daniel said.

"I haven't been able to get a band," Ashley said. "Were there any bands that tried out for prom that would work for this?"

"No . . ." I paused, thinking about Nate's band. "I don't know, maybe." The day we had auditioned bands had been a long one. Maybe we weren't hearing clearly for the last ones. "I'll find out and let you know. What about the food? Is that taken care of?"

Clarissa nodded. "That's covered."

"And the sign-up list online is looking pretty full. We might actually get a good turnout for this sober-grad-night thing," Daniel said.

"Don't sound so surprised. Other schools do this, you know."

"I just figured everyone would want to party on grad-uation night."

"We will be partying." I crossed number two off the list and tapped my pen a couple of times on the page. "So does anyone want to speak at the rally next Friday? Give the motivational 'we're about to graduate' speech?"

Daniel, who had just taken a sip from his bottle of water, coughed and tried to catch his breath. The others just stared at me.

"What?" I asked.

"We figured you'd want to speak for the last rally of the year."

"Yeah . . . Well, I'm asking if anyone else wants to."

Ashley shook her head no. As my eyes went around the table everyone else did the same. Daniel said, "Not really. You're really good at it and this was your year. You've earned it."

I wanted to feel proud about that but I wasn't sure if I should anymore. If that meant I was selfish. I had worked hard this year, mostly for college but also because I liked leadership and enjoyed giving speeches and fighting for a cause. I tapped my pen on the page a few more times. "Okay. I will. Thanks. As for the rest of the items on the agenda, just look over them and email me or Daniel with any questions. I think we'll let out early today."

The room immediately filled with chatter as everyone stood and talked between themselves. Daniel was staring at me. I didn't have to look to know.

"What?"

"You seem distracted today. Normally you're so organized and put together."

"I'm sorry."

"No, don't be. It made you more real."

I finally looked his way. "What does that mean?"

"I don't know." He glanced toward the door, where

the last person had just filed out. "I guess this whole year you've seemed a bit untouchable."

"What do you mean? We dated. How is that untouchable?"

"You were . . ." He hesitated like maybe he didn't want to hurt my feelings. "You weren't real. It's like you were the representation of what a girlfriend is supposed to be." He pointed at my binder. "The representation of what a school president is supposed to be. Picture perfect. Never a misstep. You could write the handbook."

I cringed.

He finally stood. "It's not a bad thing. But this is better. . . . It's nice. Makes me want to ask you out again."

"You already did ask me out again, and I told you I don't do repeats." I threw my pen at him as he headed for the door.

He laughed. "You're only proving my point."

I sighed and looked around the now-empty table. I'd sat here all year and what had I really done? In my binder I flipped to the tab that read *Prom*. The sign-up sheet for band auditions was still there. Twenty acts. Some were soloists, a couple of duets. The show choir had even tried out. There were nine actual bands. I wasn't sure which one was Nate's but I'd figure it out. Maybe they had a garage practice I could crash.

★ ★ ★

266

I could hear the music when I stepped out of the car. The beat of the drums reverberated through my chest as I walked up the driveway. I pasted on a smile and stepped through the side door. No one saw me at first and the song kept going, its beat reaching all the way to my toes. The song seemed catchy. The lead singer had a good voice and was very charismatic. My eyes were drawn to him as he bounced around, singing into a microphone. I repeated his name several times in my head so I would remember it—Marcus.

I hadn't stood there long when the drums stopped, Nate catching my eye with a questioning look. The other instruments kept playing but one by one each person stopped and eventually all eyes were on me.

"This is a closed rehearsal," Marcus said. If he knew who I was—the girl who had indirectly insulted his band just a couple of months ago—he didn't let on.

"I know. I was hoping to talk to you about possibly playing for sober grad."

He laughed once. "Is this a joke?"

"No." I held a clipboard as if that would make me look more professional, but I realized it probably also made it look like he was one of many bands I was considering. He was the only one. "You tried out for prom."

"And you and your friends passed. I think we'll pass this time."

So he hadn't forgotten.

The other members, even Nate, nodded in agreement and the bass player said, "The sound equipment you guys had set up that day and at prom sucked. Hard. Metallica would've sucked playing on your equipment."

"Who's Metallica?"

Marcus grunted. "You're the person in charge of music? Seriously, what have we done to deserve this form of punishment? How are you qualified to pick a band?"

"I'm not. At all."

He opened his mouth as if he were going to argue but then paused before saying, "Exactly."

"But I liked what I heard tonight. Will you play for sober grad night? Please. I came here to personally extend an invite."

He looked me up and down and I wished Nate would say something, stick up for me, but he seemed to be letting Marcus call the shots. I didn't blame him. "I don't know. I have to talk to the band. Maybe."

"Will you text me and let me know?" I handed him a card with my number on it.

He stared at it then shoved it in his back pocket. "Gia Montgomery is giving me her phone number. Wow."

"If you guys won't play . . . maybe you can refer us to a band that will because, as you pointed out, I am so not qualified to pick one."

"Sure."

"Thanks." I reached out to shake his hand and he gave me a fist bump. "How long have you all been playing together?"

"Two years."

"Do you write your own music?"

"We do."

"Well, I can tell you work hard. Thanks again." I headed for the door.

"Bye, Gia," Nate called. I smiled and left. When I was almost to my car, I heard someone call after me. I turned around to see Marcus stroll up.

"Hey, we'll think about sober grad, okay?"

I smiled. "I know, you already said that."

"But this time I mean it."

"Oh."

"See ya." And with that he walked away.

CHAPTER 31

• • • • • • •

For the first time in as long as I could remember, I didn't invite Claire and Laney over to help me get ready for my date with Hayden. If this was a real date. His sister had basically forced him to ask me to the play. She was most likely still working on her agenda of keeping Eve away from him. I even thought Bec might tag along with us, but when he showed up Friday night without Bec and kissed my hand at the door, I began to think that maybe it really was a date.

"You look gorgeous, as always, Gia."

"Thank you. You do too."

"You think I'm gorgeous?"

"I did handpick you out of a parking lot to play my date. You think I would've handpicked just any guy?"

"Well, now here's where that sends a mixed message. 'Handpicking' implies there were many to choose from. There was just me. So yes, I think you would've picked just any guy."

"Then I guess I was lucky you were gorgeous."

"Yeah, you were."

I shoved his arm and he laughed.

There was no other physical contact all the way to the theater, and when I had convinced myself again that he had just invited me along as a friend, we entered the low-lit theater and he linked hands with me. My heart gave a jump of happiness. He pointed out some seats in the middle section and we made our way there. We were sidestepping down the aisle when someone called his name.

We both turned toward the voice, and Spencer, his friend from the party, waved. "Is there an extra seat down there?" he asked.

Hayden nodded and Spencer joined us, taking the seat on the other side of Hayden when we sat down.

"Hi. It's Gia, right?"

"Yes. Hi again."

Back to Hayden he asked, "Did you see Eve?"

Hayden gestured with his head. "Yes, she's a few rows back."

Eve was here? Bec probably knew she'd come to this. So this was all another act?

No. I couldn't let myself think that way. Just because I wasn't sure of Bec's motivations didn't mean I couldn't trust Hayden's. He wanted me here. We weren't pretending tonight. It was just a coincidence that Eve was here. Except . . . he'd pretended for me when we coincidentally ran into Jules in front of the ice cream shop. Was that what was happening now? Was that why he grabbed my hand? Even with that thought, I wasn't willing to let go this time. I squeezed his hand harder. He caught my eye, and squeezed back.

Spencer craned his neck around. "Where's Ryan?"

"You know how he feels about these things."

"Don't we all feel that way?" He clapped Hayden on the back. "Oh, right, except you. You actually like watching people sing and dance. I forgot."

"You don't have to be here, Spencer." Hayden's voice was light, but I couldn't help remember what Bec had said about all his friends liking different things than he did. Why was Spencer here anyway?

"You know I'm just messing with you. You've conditioned me. But I'm not used to sitting next to you during these things. I'm used to watching you."

Hayden said something I couldn't hear to Spencer, who laughed. Then Hayden turned back to me. "You're going to love this."

"I'm sure I will." I looked at the program Spencer held. "*Into the Woods*. Like the movie?"

He let out a growl. "It was a play first."

"Is it scary?"

"It's a fairy-tale mash-up."

The lights went dark and the orchestra started to play. A spotlight lit up the curtains and they parted. Hayden flipped my hand palm up on his knee and began running a slow finger up and down each of my fingers. My nerves were so heightened that the hairs on the back of my neck stood on end. I laid my head on his shoulder. He smelled amazing—like body spray and laundry detergent. If he was trying to make it impossible to watch the show he had brought me to, he was doing a really good job of it. By the time intermission had rolled around I was so caught up in the moment of being here with Hayden that I'd almost forgotten other people were watching the show with us. The loud applause brought me out of my daze.

When the house lights came on, I sat up. "That was awesome."

Hayden smiled his full smile. "I'm glad you liked it."

"So . . . why aren't you up there?"

His jaw tightened and then loosened again. "There was a lot going on during tryouts."

"Yes, being a recluse is hard work."

His smile was back. "My sister has gotten in your head, I see," he said, not denying the observation. "So intermission is only about fifteen minutes, but now would be the time for a bathroom break if you need one. They also sell cookies and drinks in the lobby. Did you want anything?"

"I think I'm good."

"Okay, well, I have to use the restroom. I'll be back." His hand, which had found mine again, slipped free. I already couldn't wait to be holding it again.

"Okay." I took a few deep breaths, trying to return my heart rate to normal. I picked up the program and started leafing through it. There were pictures of each cast member, what role they played, and where they had performed before. Spencer slid into the seat next to me and I realized I was being rude. I quickly shut the program and smiled at him. "Hi again." I stuffed the program under my seat and pointed at the stage. "So can Hayden sing like that too?"

"He can."

"I can't wait to see him perform sometime. How long have you and Hayden known each other?"

"For years."

"Where did you meet?"

"At school." He leaned a little closer and lowered his voice. "So I have a question for you."

"Okay."

"I have this baseball fundraiser coming up. I'm not trying to win back a girlfriend or anything but it would be so nice not to go stag for once. You know how guys are. They're relentless with the jokes afterward. I don't hear the end of it for weeks. But I don't want to have to deal with actual relationship drama and expectations that come with asking out someone who I have to see all the time."

Was he asking what I thought he was asking? "I'm . . . I'm here with Hayden. Your friend."

"I know. But he told me your arrangement and it's obviously working." He nodded his head back and I slowly turned around.

Behind us, Hayden and Eve were talking. Her arm was hooked around his and she laughed at something he said. He had a big smile on his face too.

"He wanted her back. You helped him get her back. So, anyway, my thing, it would probably be three hours, tops. How much would you charge for something like that?"

I stopped cold. "What?"

"Just a date. Nothing afterward." His eyebrows went

up then down. "Unless you wanted to do something after."

I slapped him so hard that my palm stung.

"Ouch. What was that for?" He cradled his cheek.

"You haven't changed at all." He was still the same guy who had taken Laney out two years ago and treated her badly. I stood and stumbled backward and away from him. I made it out to Hayden's car only to find it locked.

I closed my eyes and counted to ten because I felt tears coming. I succeeded in keeping them at bay and sank to the curb. My phone showed a missed call from Bradley. I hesitated for one second, looked back at the empty theater entrance, then pushed Call Back.

CHAPTER 32

. . . .

Bradley answered on the second ring. "That was the longest game of phone tag ever," he said.

"It was."

"How are you?"

I thought hearing his voice again would stir something in me, make me remember what we had. Maybe even make me feel better. But it actually made my stomach hurt even more. "I'm okay. How about you?"

"I miss you like crazy, Gia."

"Really?" It was nice to hear that *someone* was thinking about me.

"You've handled this breakup way more maturely than I thought you would."

"Um . . . thanks?"

"I just mean that I expected a million texts defending yourself but instead I got silence."

"I'm sorry."

"No, that's a good thing."

Right. Nothing like silence to rekindle a connection.

"And I saw your tweet. You walked into prom and faced your friends alone. You showed so much maturity in that."

"I didn't. Not really. A friend of mine actually ended up going in with me." But were we really even friends? Was what Spencer just said true? I was surprised Hayden had told Spencer at all about the fake-date thing without warning me. Especially after he'd come and sat with us. Hayden should've warned me that Spencer knew. When had he told him anyway? Tonight?

Bradley kept talking. His voice made me remember how easy our relationship had been. Uncomplicated. There weren't ex-girlfriends to contend with or feelings to decipher or roles to be played. We had just been together.

Silence took over the line and I realized he was waiting for me to respond to something I hadn't heard. "I'm sorry. What?"

"I want to see you again."

"You do?"

"Yes."

Hayden and the way he'd been standing so close to Eve, laughing with her, flashed through my mind. "Can I ask you a question?"

"Of course."

"What did you like about me?" I was feeling very unlikable.

"You're fun. We had a lot of good times together." That was all he said. Then he stopped like that was profound and should be enough to send me running back to him. Not that I was judging him. I was pretty sure that would've been my answer if he had presented me with the same question.

"We did have fun but you were embarrassed by me."

"I was not."

"You didn't want to meet my friends and you never let me meet yours. That hurt, Bradley."

"Wow," he said. "You're . . . different."

What was I thinking? Bradley wasn't the answer to the hurt I was feeling over what Hayden had just done. "I think I am. I have to go."

"Wait, Gia."

"I can't do this. I have to go." I hung up the phone then looked toward the theater entrance. I wasn't sure what to do. I guess I'd thought Hayden would come after me, but he hadn't. He was too busy trying to win Eve back. Maybe I should've let him explain himself, but right now I was so angry and there was no way I was walking back in there with Spencer and Eve waiting in the wings.

I wasn't familiar with this part of town, but I saw a bus stop on the corner, several people waiting indicating it might actually be coming soon. I slid off my heels and walked toward it. The bus took five minutes to arrive, plenty of time for Hayden to come looking for me. He didn't. So when the bus came, the words *Beach Front* scrolling along its digital screen, I climbed on. I only had a five-dollar bill and the bus driver grumbled while he produced change for me.

I sat next to a woman with earphones in, hoping that meant she wouldn't try to talk to me, and concentrated on not crying for ten minutes.

My phone vibrated with an incoming call from Hayden that I ignored. Next came a text. I was almost too scared to look but I did.

Where are you?

I didn't answer, not sure what to say. A stupid tear dripped down my face. I swiped at it angrily.

That's when the woman next to me decided to stop ignoring me. She took out her earbuds. "Are you okay?"

"Yes, I'm fine."

"Did you know those two words make up the most-told lie in the English language?"

With those words I choked on a sob.

"Oh, sweetheart, don't cry." She awkwardly patted my arm.

"I'm fine," I said again.

She laughed a little. "Please don't add to the misuse of that phrase."

My phone chimed again. I thought you were in the bathroom. And I started to think you were dying in there, so I sent someone in to look for you. She said the bathroom was empty. Spencer said you were upset when you left. Where are you, Gia?

The woman sitting next to me still looked concerned.

"Just boy problems," I finally said, hoping she'd leave me alone. But that started her on a monologue about the problems with teenage boys today.

If you don't answer, I'm going to call the police. I'm worried.

I quickly typed. **Since you told your friend I was a hooker, I thought maybe you had the wrong idea about us. I didn't realize that was the role I was supposed to play tonight. I found a ride home.**

The phone almost immediately started ringing again. I didn't want to talk about this on the phone with a woman sitting next to me who apparently thought boys should be issued shock collars when they turned thirteen. And besides, for all I knew Hayden was calling to tell me that I was reacting like a girlfriend and not a first date. I *was* reacting like a girlfriend. I was not his girlfriend.

"I can see I'm not helping," the woman finally said.

"Thank you for trying, really." The bus stopped and I stood and walked down the aisle. I smelled the ocean the second I stepped out. The breeze and the sound of waves crashing only served as a secondary confirmation of where I was.

It was only eight o'clock so I had four hours to pout on the beach before I had to figure out how I was really getting home.

I'd only been there an hour when my phone vibrated with a text.

Did you know your parents have a GPS tracker in your phone?

CHAPTER 33

• • • • • • •

I turned around and saw a figure walking down the beach toward me. It was too dark to make out his features from this far away, but considering the text I'd just gotten, I was sure it was Hayden. I steeled my emotions. There was no way he could know how much I was hurting.

"Do you think I'm creepy *now*?" he asked when he reached me.

"Maybe more than when you waited in the parking lot to make sure I was okay."

"Understandably. This actually required effort and ingenuity. And convincing your parents that you weren't lost while simultaneously asking them to tell me where you were." He sat down next to me and studied my face. I wasn't sure what he was looking for there but it took everything in me to make sure he didn't find it.

"I want to hear your side," Hayden said. "I want to understand what happened."

"My side? What about your side?"

"My side is pretty simple. I went to use the bathroom. My ex-girlfriend pulled me into a conversation with an old friend. Then when I came back with a surprise chocolate chip cookie for you, you were gone."

"That's a pretty good side, but the side I was referring to was how exactly you explained *us* to Spencer."

He looked up like he was thinking. "Oh. After Eve's graduation party I told him how I'd met you and how you returned the favor."

"Well, he got the wrong impression."

"What do you mean? Does this have to do with the confusing hooker text you sent me?"

"I'm sure Spencer told you what happened."

"Spencer told me that you saw me talking to Eve, got really mad, said a few choice words, then left."

My jaw dropped. "That's what he said?"

"That is what he said." He took a deep breath. "Can I ask you a question?"

"Yes."

"Had you met Spencer before Eve's party?"

Oh no, this was not the right time for this to come out.

He closed his eyes for a moment as if he was disappointed by whatever shock I could feel written on my face.

"No. I mean, just once. Barely. I didn't even think he remembered me. Listen, I didn't even see you talking to Eve tonight until he pointed it out. And he only pointed it out after asking me if I'd go to some baseball banquet with him so he didn't have to go alone. He said that you told him about our *arrangement* and he was wondering how much I charged."

"He said that?"

"Yes, then he told me that he didn't need any after-date action unless I was interested."

"I did not ever tell him I paid you."

"Well, then he formed that opinion all on his own."

"That's not what he told me happened tonight."

"Of course he didn't. I'm sure he didn't want you to be mad at him."

"He said the same thing about you when I asked him

about your text. He said you were making up a story so
that I wouldn't be mad at you for acting jealous. He said
you're still mad at him for not asking Laney out for a
second date two years ago."

"Oh, please. I'm glad he didn't ask Laney out again.
He's a jerk."

Hayden still looked skeptical. He didn't believe me.
I could feel tears welling up and I bit the inside of my
cheek. "Why would I make up a story?"

"Why would *he*?"

"Because he saw what happened to your friendship
with Ryan when he betrayed you."

He narrowed his eyes. "Are you trying to say this situation is the same as what happened with Eve, Ryan, and
me?"

"No, not at all." I wiped at an errant tear, angry I had let
it escape. "I'm just trying to figure out why he would lie."

"Me too. And I want to believe you, Gia. I really do."

"Wanting to believe me and believing me are two
entirely different things."

"It's just, his story matches up more than yours. If he
did what you're saying he did, why would you run out?
Why wouldn't you come talk to me? Come tell me?"

"Because after he said what he did, I told him I was
there with you and he said that it looked like you were
there with Eve. That's when I looked back and saw you

with her. And yes, I did get jealous. But then your friend told me he wanted to fool around with me so I slapped him and left."

"I want to believe you."

"You already said that."

"Because it's true."

"Then believe me."

He sighed. "It's just he's my best friend and you seem to have a history of . . ." He didn't finish and it took me several long moments to realize how he planned on finishing.

My face went numb with disbelief. "Lying?"

He nodded.

I couldn't stop the tears now and I hated them. I hated him for having this much power over my emotions. And I hated that he got to see that after what he was saying to me. I stood and pulled out my phone as I did, turning my back to him.

"Where are you going?" Hayden asked.

"Home." I dialed the number and listened to it ring. Finally my dad picked up. "Hey, Dad. Can you come get me?" My throat burned with emotion as I successfully stopped the tears from flowing.

"Of course."

Hayden said from behind me, "I'll give you a ride home."

To my dad I said, "I'm at the Beachfront downtown."

"I'll be right there."

"Thank you." I hung up and slid the phone into my pocket.

Hayden was beside me and reached out his hand. I took a step away. This hurt worse than any breakup I'd ever experienced before and we were never even together. We hadn't even kissed. This is what it felt like to let someone in, I realized, and to really get to know them, to really let them know you. This is how it felt to genuinely like someone and to have him turn his back on you. I never wanted anyone to have this much power over my emotions again. It was safer to keep to myself, to keep things on the surface. Things ended better that way.

We stared at the ocean in silence for a long time. He probably just wished he could leave, but the gentleman in him would wait here until my dad showed up.

"For the record, I may be a lot of things—selfish, shallow, snobby—but prom night with you was the first time I'd ever lied to my friends. And when I wanted to tell them the truth that night, *you* kept it going. Not that I've been anxious to tell them since. And as for Spencer, he was such a huge jerk to Laney, but I hardly knew him. You liked him so I thought I'd give him the benefit of the doubt instead of tattling on him to you. My point is that I'm not a liar." I gave a humorless laugh. "I guess I can't even say that anymore after prom night, can I? I'll just add it to the list. I'm a selfish, shallow, snobby liar with a strong need for validation." Who had gotten extremely good at feeling sorry for herself lately.

"Gia, stop. You're not any of those things. I'm just confused because one of my best friends is telling me one thing and you're telling me the complete opposite. Can you understand why I might be a little conflicted?"

I finally managed to successfully control my emotions, to channel a calm, confident voice. "Yes, I can understand. And I'm sure you can understand why I can't be friends . . . or whatever this was . . . with someone who doesn't trust me. And what he . . . Spencer . . . did to me? That's not okay."

I heard my dad's car before I saw it. He needed it serviced or something. "Please don't call me."

Hayden ran a hand through his hair, his face pinched in concern, and nodded. I climbed into the passenger seat. My dad hesitated, looking at Hayden.

"Go, Dad. Please."

And he did. As soon as we rounded the corner, my shoulders fell and the tears I'd been holding back burst out of me.

"Honey?"

"I hate boys."

"He didn't hurt you, did he?" His voice was surprisingly angry.

"No, well, he just hurt my heart."

"Oh, honey." My dad reached over and, while still driving, managed to direct my head to his shoulder. "I'm so sorry. Just let it out."

And I did. Apparently my dad was easier to open up to than I'd ever realized. That thought only made me cry harder.

CHAPTER 34

• • • • • • •

"In case you were wondering," Bec said, sitting down in front of me Monday morning, "I totally believe you and I told Hayden as much."

"Thanks." Not that it mattered. I never wanted to speak to Hayden again.

"Because Spencer is a slimeball. I don't know how Hayden's friends turned out to be such jerks. I think it's because they all got to know each other as kids when they were only half jerks. I'm convinced if he had met either Spencer or Ryan in the last couple of years, he would've seen right through them."

I didn't trust my voice so I just nodded.

"Even if Spencer's story was true, I would've fully supported you marching out of there in a jealous rage too. And I told Hayden that the only thing I would've done different if he were my date and was there talking to his ex was punched him before I walked out. Why does my idiot brother keep talking to that idiot girl? Especially when he's on a date."

"We weren't on a date."

"He told me it was a date. Did he tell you it wasn't?"

"No."

"He likes you, Gia. He's just being an idiot."

"It doesn't matter. He doesn't trust me and I definitely don't trust him anymore. Considering that's the basis of all good relationships, I think we're out of luck."

Bec put her hand over mine. "My brother is extremely loyal. Sometimes to a fault. His loyalty can outweigh his reasoning. His brain was telling him one thing and his heart was telling him another. One time when I was little, he watched me shove a boy to the ground and steal his Popsicle. I told Hayden it was mine, that the boy had taken it from me first, and Hayden believed me. He told this crying kid to leave me alone. Loyalty."

"I get your point, but the problem is that in that story I'm the crying kid who got his Popsicle stolen.

I'm not the one he's loyal to."

She let out an angry sigh. "I know, but *my* point is that he has it wrong. He should've given the kid back his Popsicle and told me I was a bully."

I laughed. "Well, that means a lot to me."

"Will you talk to him?"

"He doesn't want to talk, Bec. He wants Eve back. I'm sorry I failed in your mission, but they can have each other."

"My mission?"

"The whole reason you want me to talk to him again. You hate Eve."

"I can't deny that point. But no, I like you, Gia." She grabbed my forearm and met my eyes with her black-lined ones. "No matter how much I tried to convince myself not to, I actually like you."

Those words made me want to both laugh and cry at the same time. "I like you too but I don't have to make up with your brother for that to continue."

"I think you and my brother are good together. You make him more confident and he makes you more relaxed. When you find someone like that, you don't let them go so easily."

I gave a small laugh. "Well, thanks, Dr. Phil, but it's over and I don't do repeats."

★ ★ ★

I didn't feel like going out to lunch with my friends. I didn't feel like doing anything but sitting in my fourth-period class and not moving ever again. Somehow I stood up, though, shouldered my backpack, and found Claire.

"What's wrong?" she asked immediately. That morning on the car ride over I'd done a pretty good job of hiding my sadness. But somehow talking to Bec made everything worse. Her believing me made it even more sad that Hayden hadn't. Made me realize even more that he should've.

"Bad day."

"You want to talk about it?"

"Not really."

"Is it Drew? Are you guys still fighting?"

"Yes—wait, how did you know Drew and I were fighting?" I hadn't told anyone else because that would require them having to watch the most embarrassing video ever.

"Jules said she saw some video online or something."

"She did? How?"

"I don't know. Maybe your brother linked it on his Facebook page. Anyway, she said you were mad at Drew. I thought you told her that. I was surprised you hadn't told *me*."

"No, I didn't tell her." I couldn't process what that meant. That she was still sneaking around looking for answers? That, like Claire, she thought my brother was cute and had friended him on Facebook?

"So is that why you're upset?" Claire asked.

"No." Maybe talking to Claire would help. "Remember that guy I went on a blind date with?"

"Yes."

"We kind of broke up."

"I didn't know you were together."

"We weren't but I wanted to be."

"I'm sorry, Gia. First Bradley and now Hayden. That's not cool."

"No, it isn't." We were in the parking lot now and I could see Jules and Laney waiting by the car. "Can we just keep this between you and me for now?" I asked, not wanting to deal with prying questions from Jules today. Especially since it seemed like she was doing just that—prying.

"Why? We're all your friends, Gia. We want to help you through it. You need to stop keeping things from us."

"I just can't handle Jules right now. Please."

"For the life of me I don't understand why the two of you don't get along."

"Really? You don't see how she is with me? She is

constantly trying to pick apart my stories for some hidden agenda."

"Yes, I can see how she does that sometimes, but she's said the same about you before."

"Well, she started it." It sounded juvenile before it was out of my mouth. I didn't need Claire's eye roll to confirm it.

"Just try. She's been through a lot."

"I did try and she didn't care."

"Try more than once. She's moving in with me for the rest of year because her mom is running from some guy again."

I swallowed hard. "She's moving in with you?"

"Yes, and I need my two best friends to get along."

The one time I'd tried to do something nice for Jules by inviting her to my house for our pre-date ritual she ended up lying about it. I stopped, realizing what I'd just said in my head. The one time. There was the ice cream store attempt too, but that wasn't me really going out of my way. Claire was right. I really hadn't tried very hard. I rarely made the effort to reach out to her. If Claire liked her, then there must've been something I was missing. Something I wasn't trying very hard to see. I hooked my arm in Claire's, laid my head on her shoulder, and said, "Okay, I'll try."

"Gia gets to pick the restaurant today," Claire said

as she was unlocking the doors. "Her almost boyfriend broke up with her."

Jules craned her head toward me. "Which boyfriend?"

"Hayden."

"Is it because he saw you hanging out with Bradley?"

I took a breath to find some patience before I responded. From Jules's side that was true. The last time she'd seen me, I *was* hanging out with "Bradley." "No, that's not why. His friend was being a slime bag and he didn't believe me."

"That sucks," Laney said.

"Yes, it really does." I got in the front seat and clicked the seat belt in place.

Jules placed a hand on my shoulder from the backseat. "I'm sorry about Hayden."

I smiled. She sounded so sincere. Maybe when I'd chased her down outside the coffee shop, she realized I really was interested. Maybe it had been me all along who was holding our friendship back. I could try harder. I would. We'd be fine.

Claire started the car. "Where to?"

"In-N-Out."

It took me a second to recognize him out of context like this, walking into the restaurant as I sat there with Claire, Laney, and Jules. I was facing the door and my first thought was, *That guy looks familiar.* Then I nearly spilled my chocolate milk shake as I got to my feet. "Drew?"

He smiled at me then headed over. When he reached me he gave me a hug. "I should've asked permission to make the video."

That still wasn't an apology but it made me smile. "What are you doing here?"

"I decided I needed to see you."

My friends were staring at me so I said, "Drew, you remember Claire and Laney and this is Jules. This is my brother."

"Good to finally meet you in real life," he said to Jules.

"What does that mean?" I asked.

"We met online a couple of days ago. She said I'd want her help with something."

Why did that news send dread into my heart? "I thought you hated the internet."

He smiled like it was a joke.

"Help with what?"

"You'll see."

"How did you know I was here?" I asked him.

"Mom and Dad have a GPS in your phone. Tell me you knew that."

"I know. I just don't know why they insist on giving that information out to everyone."

"Because I brought you a surprise. A make-up gift. Something your friend assured me you'd be happy about." With that he smiled at Jules and the dread in my heart turned to ice.

"A make-up gift?"

"A present to make up for my extremely horrible behavior."

I smiled nervously. If Jules was involved, this couldn't be good . . . or maybe Claire had been giving her the "try harder" speech too. Maybe she really was trying harder. Maybe she'd watched that video Drew made and realized my life was hard sometimes too. This was the first burst of hope I'd had in an otherwise awful day. My brother had come and was extending a peace offering. A peace offering from both him and Jules.

"Are you ready?"

"Yes."

He smiled like he was the one getting the gift, went back to the door, and opened it. In walked Bradley. Not fill-in Bradley. The real-life, honest-to-goodness, in-the-flesh Bradley. I'd forgotten how beefy he was. His arms seemed huge. Too big. Had I liked that at one point? His hair was perfectly arranged, his smile perfect and white, and he must've been to the tanning bed because his skin was darker than ever.

Drew was walking slightly behind him and had a big,

proud smile on his face like he had just brought me a pile of money or something.

"Gia," Bradley said, then scooped me up in a lung-crushing hug. He was going to break my spine with his comically large arms. Then he set me down and turned toward my friends. This was all happening entirely too fast and my brain was having trouble keeping up. So when he said, "I'm Brad—" my scream of "No!" was one second too late.

The flash of vindication in Jules's eyes let me know this was the plan.

"Wait. You're Bradley?" Laney asked. "UCLA Bradley?"

"That's me. And see, Gia, I'm not embarrassed by you. I'm here to finally meet your friends. It's long overdue." He kissed my cheek and I had to physically stop myself from wiping it when he pulled away.

Claire had a look on her face like . . . well, like I had been lying to her for the last month. "Gia? What?"

"He broke up with me in the parking lot at prom. But he exists. See?"

"So, what? You just called a friend to pretend to be him?"

"You had someone pretend to be me?" Bradley asked.

My shoulders started to shake and I had to wrap my arms around myself to stop them. "I just needed to extend the night a little bit. You were there. You were supposed to go inside with me, not break up with me."

Bradley closed his eyes like he had made the biggest mistake in the world coming here today. I really wished he hadn't.

"Really, Gia?" Drew said.

I pointed at Jules. "She was trying to prove Bradley didn't exist." I had become a child. It was pointless now. I'd dug myself a grave and I was being buried alive in it. "She did this."

"So you lied to us?" Claire asked.

"I'm sorry. I really, truly am. I didn't mean to lie. Bradley exists. He just left me in the parking lot, so I felt like it really wasn't a huge lie. I just rearranged the order of how things happened . . . with a fill-in guy."

"So who was that fill-in guy?" Claire asked.

"She still called him Bradley when I ran into them at the ice cream shop the other day." Jules was loving every second of this. She'd worked hard for this payday and it was probably going exactly like she'd imagined it.

"That was Hayden."

"Blind-date Hayden? So that really wasn't a blind date, then. You obviously already knew him."

"Yes."

"So *that* time did you mean to lie?" Claire's words were ice cold.

"I messed up."

"You think?" Laney said quietly.

"Why, Gia?" Claire asked.

"Because I was scared."

"Of what?" It felt like it was just Claire and me now. Her icy stare from before turned sad.

"Jules didn't think Bradley existed. I thought that . . ." I trailed off because it sounded so lame now.

"I'd believed you all along about Bradley."

"I know. I just thought you wouldn't that night. I thought it would be the last piece of evidence you needed from her to prove I was a liar."

"You proved you were a liar pretty easily all on your own."

My heart sank even further. "I know."

"Why didn't you trust in our friendship?"

"I don't know. Maybe because my relationships have always been so surface. I haven't really been myself. Ever. I never let anyone in." I knew it was the wrong thing to say the moment it came out of my mouth but it was too late to take it back. "That came out wrong. I didn't know they were only surface. I thought we had a great relationship until I realized what it was like to really open up." I closed my eyes. I was only making this worse. "I'm sorry."

Claire stood. "Glad to know how you feel." With that

she left. Laney paused for one brief moment and then went with her.

I looked at Drew, but he just shook his head in disgust. He was now probably very pleased with himself for making a video about how much I needed validation. "Really, Gia?"

"Please don't judge me right now." My voice wobbled when I spoke so I didn't say anything else.

He tapped Bradley's arm and jerked his head toward the door and they both walked away. Why didn't I have a brother who would defend me even if I stole a Popsicle? I leaned my forehead on the table and decided I wasn't moving until someone made me.

Someone clearing her throat made me look up. How had I not noticed that Jules hadn't left with the others?

"What?"

"I've been to six high schools in four years. Claire was the only person who ever made me feel like I belonged."

"So that's what it was always about? You wanted to steal Claire from me?"

"I just knew she deserved better."

Jules was right. Claire did deserve better than me. I put my forehead back on the table and listened as Jules clicked her way out of the restaurant on her high heels. For the second time in as many days, I realized I needed to call my dad for a ride home. I was stranded.

★ ★ ★

The problem with having the only person I could really talk to right now be the sister of the person I didn't want to see ever again was that I was stuck in a car trying to figure out things on my own. It used to be that I could do that really well, back at the beginning of the year. And despite how many people had told me lately that I was different and better and changed, I sure felt lost and angry and alone. I just wanted my old self back. The one who could force a problem away until she could deal with it. But maybe that was the problem—I never ended up dealing with anything.

Something Jules of all people had said stuck in my head. Claire deserved better. She was right. Claire deserved better than a friend like Jules. And I truly thought I could be better. . . . I was better. Better than the stupid lie I'd told over a month ago. Better than the person I'd been at the beginning of the year who didn't think much about other people aside from how they could help me. I hadn't even realized I had been that person until now.

I started my car and drove to Claire's house. I had to deal with this. I'd screwed up. I knocked on her front door, and her mom, who usually invited me in with a smile, positioned her body to block the way.

"I'm sorry, Gia. She doesn't want to talk to you right now."

I thought about that doormat her mom had bought for us that claimed it wasn't a doormat and how Claire was applying its statement in this moment. I wanted to put a smile on my face, to pretend like everything was or at least would be perfect. Instead I said, "I've been a horrible friend. Will you tell her that? There's no excuse for what I did. Will you just tell her I'm sorry and that maybe she can talk to me one day soon? And will you tell her 'eighty-three days'?"

Her mom nodded then shut the door.

I wasn't sure she would tell her all that so I texted it to Claire and my little thought about the doormat and how I was glad she wasn't letting me get away with my bad behavior but how I hoped she'd forgive me one day. Finally I texted the amount of days until we would be roommates.

The only thing she texted back was **We still have thirty days to change roommate preferences.**

I stared at that text, standing on the front porch of her house, hoping she wasn't implying what I thought she was implying. Jules had won. She'd wanted Claire and she'd gotten her.

I swallowed down the lump in my throat.

At home I thought it would be awkward. That my parents would be angry with me. But I should've known better. I walked into the house and found my parents and Drew sitting around the kitchen table and talking. I waited for the angry exclamations but all I got was my dad saying, "Gia, lying is never the answer."

I waited for more. For anger. Drew grunted like for the last couple of hours he'd been trying to get them riled up over my actions.

"You should've seen how they defended you," I said.

"We stand behind both our children," my mom said.

"It's easier to see our mistakes if you face us," Drew said.

My mom smiled at him like it was a joke, like she thought he was so clever.

"I'm going to my room," I said, knowing this was going nowhere. My parents were well set in their ways.

"You're grounded," Drew called after me.

"Only if you are."

CHAPTER 35

• • • • • • •

I awoke to humming. Off-key humming. I cracked one
eye open and saw my mom putting stacked clothes of
folded laundry on my dresser.

"You should be awake," she said.

I pulled my pillow over my head. "I'm not going to
school today."

"Yes, you are."

"Mom, I don't want to. I had a bad day yesterday."

"You can't hide from your problems."

"Why not? You do."

The room became so silent that I thought maybe she

had left. I moved my pillow to see her standing in the middle of my room, staring out my window, a look of sadness on her face. I wanted to take back what I'd said, but I didn't.

"You can use Dad's car today," she said, then turned and left my room.

I somehow got myself showered and ready for school. I went to the kitchen to eat breakfast with my mom like I always did, thinking I could apologize, but she wasn't there . . . like she always was. Instead there was a note on the counter. *Went to work early. There's cereal in the pantry.*

Drew stumbled into the kitchen after me and read the note over my shoulder. "You broke Mom."

I clenched my teeth. "*You* broke Mom." I pushed past him, grabbed the keys off the hook in the laundry room, and left the house.

Drew was right. I'd broken everything, but today I was going to fix it. So when I pulled into the lot, I parked in the section where Claire always did. Her car wasn't there. I waited with no luck until the bell rang. The second bell didn't magically produce her either. My eyes drifted to Laney's car, parked a few rows over. Had they driven together? I knew I needed to fix things with Laney and Jules as well, but I wanted to start with Claire.

I sighed and climbed out of my car. As I headed to

class, an idea took over. I was student body president. I usually didn't abuse that title, but today I was going to make it work for me. I changed my direction and went to the front office.

If I acted like this was normal, it would work. I pasted on a smile and approached Mrs. Fields. "Hi, I'm working on last-minute details for the rally this Friday and I need to borrow Claire Dunning from her first-period class."

"What class is she in?" Mrs. Fields asked like I did this all the time.

"Calculus. Freeman."

My heart raced, but it must not have shown because she picked up the phone and dialed. "Hi," she said after a moment. "I need Claire in the front office please." She gave a few hums then hung up. I waited for her to tell me that Claire wasn't at school today.

She didn't. She smiled up at me and said, "She's on her way."

"Oh. Great. I'll just wait outside for her. Thanks so much." I stepped out the door and tried to think of what I was going to say. There was no excuse for what I had done. What I'd said. That would be a good opening line. There really wasn't. If I were Claire, I'd be mad too. But we'd been best friends for ten years—that fact had to count for something.

I heard her shoes on the cement before I saw her round

the corner. Her calm, curious look immediately hardened when she saw me. Then she stopped in the middle of the hall still forty feet away. I didn't hesitate to close the gap between us.

"Can we just talk?"

"Did you seriously just call me out of class for this? Did you *lie* to Mrs. Fields to get me here?"

Maybe that wasn't such a good idea. "No. Yes, but just barely." What was wrong with me? I went with my preplanned line. "There's no excuse for what I've done."

"For lying to get me out of class?"

"No . . . well, maybe that too, but actually I think wanting to talk to you is a halfway decent excuse." I shook my head. "I'm talking about lying to you about Bradley."

"I know what you're talking about." Her expression hadn't softened at all. "Is that all?" She started to back away.

"No. And for what I said at the restaurant. I didn't mean we've never been friends. You're my best friend, Claire. I've been so selfish. I just want to talk about this. I messed up and I wanted to say sorry."

"Well, you said it." She turned and headed back up the hall.

"That's it?" I called after her. "I'm trying to fix this."

She didn't turn back around.

Time. I knew she just needed time. I'd hurt her and she wasn't going to get over it that quickly. That's what I was telling myself to hold it together. But when I heard two girls whisper the word "liar" when they passed me during break later that day, I couldn't handle it anymore. I marched straight to the portables and found Bec.

"I need you," I said, pulling her up by the arm and back through the crowded hallways toward the parking lot.

"Be careful. The whole school is seeing this."

"I'm having a breakdown." My chest was tight and I barely squeezed the words out.

She pressed her darkened lips together. "So . . . you want to go throw some baseballs? I actually drove to school today."

"Yes," I said without a second's thought.

"Cool. Let's go."

As Bec drove toward the old country house, she hummed a song that was playing on the radio. After several minutes she said out of nowhere, "Do you believe in second chances?"

"No," I said immediately because I knew she was talking about Hayden.

"So you don't think Claire should give you a second chance?"

I sighed. "Yes, I do."

"I do too." That's all she said. I wasn't sure if she meant that she thought Claire should give me a second chance or if she was just saying that she believed in them in general.

I was tired of talking about me, of thinking about my problems. I needed a break from them. "How is Nate? What's going on there? Have you told him you're madly in love with him?"

"Am I? Madly in love with him, I mean? I'm not sure that I am. That would be the only kind of love that would make me want to tell him at this point. The kind that would drive me to do something crazy like that. The mad kind."

"Why is it crazy to tell him?"

"Because he's a great friend. I don't want to make that weird. You know?"

"Yeah, I know. Losing friends is the worst."

"Hayden's a mess, Gia."

I groaned. We had changed the subject. She wasn't allowed to change it back.

"Here's the thing—"

"Please, I don't want to talk about it."

"Just hear me out and then I'll shut up."

"Fine."

She nodded once. "Thank you. So here's the thing,"

she said again with a smirk in my direction. "He didn't want to be Ryan. He didn't want to choose a girl over a friend. He had just been on the wrong end of that and knew how it felt and he didn't want to do it to someone else. To the only friend he had left after everything with Eve blew up. He needed to believe Spencer. But it doesn't matter anymore because he confronted him. Like, really confronted him and the truth about you came out. And he's a mess, Gia."

"He hasn't tried to call or text or anything."

"Because he screwed up and he knows it. He doesn't think he deserves a second chance. So please, you have to talk to him."

"I shouldn't have to be the one to initiate this."

"I know, believe me, I know. But you told him not to call you. And now he's playing the 'I don't deserve her' card. I swear, I don't know if all actors are this dramatic or just him but I'm ready to kill him. You have to forgive him before he drives me insane."

"But I don't know if I do forgive him."

"Fine. I guess I have to kill both of you, then." She pulled up the long dirt drive of Will's house. We passed the truck we had thrown baseballs at last time and I thought maybe this trip was a bad idea after all because the memories came pouring in.

The four big dogs surrounded our car, barking. Bec

honked but no one came out to put them away.

"It's all you this time," she said.

"What? You really are going to kill me? I thought that was a joke."

"They won't kill you. I can't promise they won't bite you."

I looked into the backseat. "Where are the baseballs?"

"You know, I didn't think I needed to bring a bucket of balls to school this morning."

"I thought that's why we took your car. Maybe we should just leave."

"No, we're here. There are always a few we accidentally leave behind. I bet there's a couple inside our last target practice."

I chewed on my lip, watching the dogs jump up on the car.

She patted the center console. "Can I borrow your phone for a sec? Mine ran out of juice."

I dug my phone out of my pocket and handed it to her then watched her start to dial in a number. She noticed me watching, reached over, and unbuckled my seat belt. "Come on. Out."

"Fine. When these dogs maim me, I'm giving your name to the police."

She didn't respond and I stepped out of the car. The dogs immediately jumped on me, knocking me several steps backward. I caught myself on the car.

"Show them who's boss," she said, reaching over and shutting the door I'd left open.

I grabbed one by the collar and led him toward the fence. The others followed, nipping at my heels and barking. They were so loud my ears rang. I was convinced Will wasn't home or he would've thought an army was coming to rob his house. Once they were safely behind the gate, I turned with a proud smile to see that the car and Bec were gone. I walked slowly back to the road, thinking maybe she'd just parked it somewhere. I instinctively reached for my pocket to pull out my phone and remembered she'd borrowed it . . . stolen it! She'd set me up. For what I wasn't sure, but I did not have to go along with this.

With my best friendly face on, I knocked on Will's door, hoping I was wrong about him not being home. Maybe he just enjoyed watching his dogs terrorize people. His house may have looked older than dirt but he had to have a phone in there. Nobody answered. I peered through the dirt-smudged window to the right of the door and saw nothing but a darkened hallway.

How had people ever lived without cell phones? I was stuck in the middle of nowhere. I sank to the porch and put my forehead on my knees. Bec had to come back sometime. At the very least, someone would have to wonder where I was when school got out. Maybe. As I sat there, alone, I thought about what she'd said about Hayden. He was a mess, she'd said. That thought twisted my heart and for one moment I thought that maybe she was right. That I really did need to give him a second chance, give us a second chance. It's what I was asking for from Claire. How could I not offer the same thing to someone else? But as soon as that thought came, the night on the beach pressed on my shoulders. This was different from my fight with Claire. He'd called me a liar when I'd never lied to him. He didn't believe me after his friend had been a major jerk.

Anger surged through me. No. I couldn't get over what had happened so easily. My eyes zeroed in on the '68 Camaro across the yard. I pushed myself to my feet and went in search of some baseballs.

CHAPTER 36

The pile of balls I'd found littered the tall weeds by my feet. I'd found more than a couple. It took me about thirty minutes, but I'd collected at least twenty. I held one in my hand, poised to throw it at the Camaro. A memory of sitting in that car with Hayden came to my mind and I almost dropped the ball. Then another memory surged to the front to stomp it out, Bec's words from that same day: "Did you use the 'climb over me into the car' move on her?" she'd said. He'd done that with another girl. Probably Eve.

I pulled my arm back and threw the ball with all my

might. It hit the door with a loud clank then bounced off and rolled across the ground. The ding it left in the rusted door was hardly noticeable and only heightened my need to do damage. Real damage. I picked up another ball and hurled it. Then another.

Soon it wasn't just Hayden I was trying to crush but Jules and my parents, Drew and myself. I reached down for another ball and felt nothing but dirt. I had thrown them all. My heart rate was high and my cheeks were wet with sweat and maybe a few tears.

I started to gather the balls when behind me I heard, "Do you want to throw a few at the actual person those are intended for or is the car satisfying enough?"

I whirled around. Hayden held out his arms like he was really giving me permission to pelt him. It was tempting.

My shoulders rose and fell several times. After the week I'd had, I just wanted to wrap myself up in him and forget what had happened. But I couldn't. As I stood there staring at Hayden I wondered if he was playing a role right now. The calm and collected humble guy. Was he putting up a front for me? Because he didn't look like the mess Bec claimed he was. I threw the baseball I held after all. Not hard and it didn't even hit him but it almost did.

His eyes went wide with surprise.

"So you weren't really offering me a target?"

He gave a small laugh. "I didn't think you'd take me up on it."

I picked up another ball and threw it up in the air twice before I tossed it back to the dirt. He scooped up a ball by his foot and walked to my side then turned to face the car. He brought his arm back to throw and I grabbed his hand, ball and all. "No. Don't do that. You love this car."

My all-out effort had amounted to a few dings but I knew he could do some serious damage.

He relaxed his arm and let the ball fall to the ground. My hand still gripped his for two beats before I realized and let go, taking a step back to put some space between us.

"I have trust issues," he said to the ground.

"After Eve and Ryan, I'm sure you do."

"I messed up."

"I know."

"Do you want me to leave?"

"I haven't decided what I want yet."

He raised his eyebrows then went still. Like for the first time since our fight he thought that maybe there was hope for us. "What's the deciding factor?"

I tried not to smile when I remembered we'd had this conversation before on the way to Eve's party. But back then we were talking about whether I was going to call

Bradley back or not. Whether he was going to get back with Eve or not. "Right now, I guess."

He nodded slowly. "I can give you lots of reasons why you should probably just walk away."

"Oh yeah?"

"The first one being that I called you a liar when I'd been lying too."

"That's a good reason," I said.

"Yes. The second one is that I have the world's worst taste in friends."

"You seem to."

"And I'm still not sure what that says about me."

I wanted to reassure him, but I still hadn't made any decisions and reassuring him would only make him think I had.

"Plus I like you too much."

Why did that statement make my heart race?

He clenched and unclenched his fist. "And that scares me because apparently those trust issues I mentioned before extend to not even trusting myself or my feelings and that can only mean I'm going to hurt you. Again. I don't want to see you cry. It rips my heart out. I'm an idiot and I'm sorry."

I closed my eyes so I didn't have to stare at him looking so vulnerable. He was listing reasons not to like him. These weren't reasons to throw myself into his arms like my entire being seemed to want to do. "Before you," I started slowly, "I had a plan. I knew what I wanted. I thought I knew myself. I knew how every week of the next four years of my life was going to play out. But now I don't have the roommate I was supposed to have or the boyfriend or the plan. It's gone. I don't know what I want anymore."

"You don't know what you want?" His voice was husky.

I opened my eyes expecting to see him staring at me with that smoldering look he had perfected at prom but it wasn't that look. It was a soft, open look. One that wasn't an act. I shook my head. "No, I know what I want. I want to go to college, with or without the roommate I always thought I'd have."

He nodded.

"And I'm going to use my scholarship to study political science and hope that I can make a difference in the world one day."

He smiled.

I took a step toward him, and when he didn't step back, I took another. I put my hands on his shoulders. "And I want . . ."

He let out a breath, his entire being seeming to relax. "Don't do it unless you mean it," he said, repeating a line I'd used before.

I smiled. "I mean it." I took his face in my hands and pushed myself to my toes.

Before our lips met he said, "I feel like this is the biggest buildup to a kiss ever. That no matter what I do you're going to be disappointed."

I laughed. "Should we play Twenty Questions?"

"How would that work in this situation?"

"I could try to guess your preferences."

"My preferences in a kiss?"

I nodded, our faces still very close together.

"My preference is simple—you."

"That was not a yes-or-no answer. You just broke the ru—"

He cut me off by pressing his lips to mine. They were so warm that my whole body seemed to melt against him. He slipped his arms around my waist and pulled me closer, deepening the kiss as he did. My hands found his hair, not needing an excuse to touch him this time, knowing I could do this whenever I wanted.

A shiver went through me and he smiled against my lips. "So, not a disappointment?"

I didn't answer, just kissed him more.

CHAPTER 37

· · · · · · ·

We sat on the ground, our backs pressed up against the Camaro, our shoulders pressed together, tossing a baseball back and forth between his right hand and my left.

"Thank you," he said after we'd completed several catches each.

"For what?"

"For texting me. For giving me another chance."

The ball he'd just thrown me dropped onto my lap.

"What?" he asked.

"I texted you?"

"Yes."

"What exactly did I say?"

"You don't remember?"

I held out my hand. "Let me see your phone."

He shifted a little so he could get his phone out of his pocket then he handed it to me. I opened his messages and saw the text from me. It said, **Hayden, meet me at Will's place. I'll be the one destroying a car. I want to talk.**

I pursed my lips. How did Bec know I'd be attempting to destroy a car?

"I take it that wasn't from you?"

"Bec stole my phone."

He shook his head. "Normally I'd be indignant at her sneakiness but this time not so much." He planted a kiss on my lips and I crossed my leg over his, needing to be closer. He responded, slipping his hand around my waist, sending chills up my spine.

When he pulled away, he asked, "Do you know how long I've wanted to do that?"

"Well, sometime after Eve's party, I'm assuming."

He shook his head. "I wanted to at Eve's party, but I didn't think it was fair to kiss you that night when I was playing head games, when Eve was about to walk around the corner. I wanted to take my time."

"And that you did."

"You were sending me mixed messages. I wasn't

sure if you wanted me to."

"Mixed messages? How so?"

"I'd try to hold your hand, you'd let go. I'd try to get you to talk, you'd close up."

"I thought you were doing it out of duty. I didn't want to be some fake scene you were performing. Someone to practice lines on."

"Ouch."

"Sorry. I just really, really liked you."

He smiled. "Liked?"

"Like. I really, really like you." I got up on my knees and faced him. I kissed his cheek then the corner of his mouth. "We should get your sister back."

His eyes, which had been closed, popped open. "What?"

"Your sister."

"Not really who I want to think about in this moment." He pulled me onto his lap and kissed my temple then my neck.

"No, really." I pushed away a little. "She totally tricked us today."

"I thought we were happy about this."

"We are, but that doesn't mean we shouldn't get her back."

"Did you have something in mind?"

"We let her think this didn't happen." I pointed

between the two of us. "Put your beautiful acting skills to work."

He laughed. "I'm totally in. Let's start now." He got his phone and began to type. I twisted around, my back to his chest, so I could read what he wrote.

Where are you? I'm at Will's and no one is here.

"Do you think she's still on my phone and will respond to your texts as me?"

"We'll see."

His phone chimed. **You're at Will's?**

"There's your answer."

"I'm beginning to think we're having those immature brains again that your mom talked about."

"I think my mom might approve in this case."

I gestured for him to hand me his phone. He did and I took over the texts.

If you're going to play head games with me, Gia, I'm out of here.

Hayden laughed. His phone rang and I almost dropped it. Bec's name flashed on the screen. Hayden cleared his throat and turned his smiling face into a serious one.

"Hello?"

I leaned close and he angled the phone so we could both hear.

"Hayden, hi. What's going on?"

"Nothing."

"Where are you?"

He shook his head and mouthed, *She should go into acting too, right?*

I nodded in agreement.

"Nowhere. I'm actually just about to head home."

I tapped his leg. "Tell her you're going to stop by Eve's first," I whispered.

He bit his lip trying to contain a laugh. His voice didn't reflect it, though, when he said, "Eve just called. I'm going to stop by her house."

"Don't you dare. I saw Gia today."

"And? I don't really want to see her. I think she's playing games with me. She asked me to meet her somewhere and then wasn't there."

"She had a rough day. Everyone at school is gossiping about her. I think her friends must've found out about prom. You need to talk to her."

Hayden's playful act was gone as his whole face turned serious. He looked at me. My smile had disappeared too.

"I'm sorry," he said. "I had no idea."

"Don't tell me that," Bec said. "Tell her."

"I will."

"What?"

"I have to go."

He hung up to her objections then pulled me into a hug. "I'm sorry."

I shrugged. "It's fine."

"You did not just say that."

I laughed a little. "Okay, it sucks. My best friend won't talk to me."

"Claire?"

"Yes. I tried to apologize. She's really mad. Not that I blame her. I'd be mad too, but I think she doesn't want to be my roommate anymore. She and Jules are going to room together."

"No."

"Yes . . . maybe. I honestly don't know. I think she just needs some time to decide if she wants to forgive me or not."

He kissed the top of my head. "She'll forgive you."

I filled him in on the rest of my week, and with his arms around me, it all didn't seem so bad.

CHAPTER 38

• • • • • • •

Drew was sitting on the couch in the living room when I walked in the house. I sighed, not really wanting him to take away the happy feelings I had after spending the last hour making out with Hayden.

"I thought I grounded you," he said.

"After nearly eighteen years of not being grounded, I didn't know how it worked."

"Where have you been? I thought I could get clues to your whereabouts on Twitter but there's been social media silence going on thirty-six hours now. I almost sent out a search party."

"You're kind of a judgmental jerk now."

He shrugged. "I've kind of always been. I thought we were firmly in that camp together. What happened?"

"I'm trying to be a better person. Some days it works."

"So the whole lying thing? That was part of being a better person?"

"No, that's what started the journey."

"Well. Let me know how it works out and I'll decide if I'm willing to give it a try."

"So far I've lost a few friends, the whole school is giving me dirty looks, and my brother thinks I'm amoral."

"Actually your brother is kind of impressed you know what the word 'amoral' means." He pushed himself to standing. "So I'll check the no box on being a better person, then."

"On the other side, I've gained some amazing friends who actually know me and I think I know myself better."

He nodded his head like he approved. "Can I do another documentary on you?"

I picked up a couch pillow and hit him with it. "You think this is some sort of big joke? That you didn't kill me with what you did? That you can just stand here with your 'I'm too cool for everyone' attitude and think everything is fine between us?"

"I was kind of hoping."

I hit him one more time over the head with the pillow, dropped it, and sank to the couch. "You don't know everything no matter how much you act like it."

He sat down next to me. "I know."

"I don't put everything online. Especially my real feelings."

"I'm sorry."

I went still. It was the first time he'd said it, probably the only time I'd ever heard him say it.

"I'm really, truly sorry, Gia. I messed up."

I met his eyes. "So why were you trying to get me in trouble with Mom and Dad, then?"

"Because Mom and Dad . . ." He grunted in frustration. "Because they don't make us accountable for anything. It turned me into a crappy person. I was hoping they'd do better with you."

"Are you blaming Mom and Dad for your issues? How original of you."

He laughed. "I know. Everyone has issues with their parents." He tapped my knee with his fist. "I used to think you didn't."

"I used to pretend I didn't."

"Welcome to the real world, sister."

"Funny. So . . . you really hate Mom and Dad?"

"No, of course not. I've just discovered the things I agree with them about and the things I don't."

"Like the fact that they still forgive us more easily than they should," I pointed out.

Drew shrugged. "Things could be a lot worse."

"They could be judgmental jerks."

"Or lying snobs."

I turned to my brother, taking in his too-long hair and his cocky little grin. "One day you're going to meet a girl who knocks you down a few pegs. I really hope she's a Twitter addict."

"That would be a deal breaker, G."

"And that's why it will be so satisfying."

He took a deep breath. "If she's at all like you, I'll consider myself lucky."

Tears made my eyes sting, and as I was fumbling with how to respond to that, he pulled his keys out of his pocket. "Well, I have to go."

It was obvious we had a long way to go in the communicating-our-feelings department, but it felt possible now. I nodded.

"Bradley is waiting for me. We drove together up here."

"Bradley is still here?" I looked around, waiting for him to appear out of nowhere again.

"Not here but I left him at a driving range."

"Golf?"

"Yes."

"I didn't know he liked golf."

"Yeah, he doesn't know much about you either."

"It's pathetic, I know."

"What's pathetic is that I am going to be stuck driving with him for the next three hours and we have absolutely nothing in common."

I laughed and gave him a hug. "Thanks for the thought. Thanks for . . . Thanks."

Five minutes after my brother left, my mom walked in the front door. She paused when she saw me then quickly replaced her open mouth of surprise with a smile. "Gia, hi. You're home."

I stood. "Mom, no need to pretend you're not upset. I was really mean to you this morning and I'm sorry."

"It's okay. We're good. It's fine." She headed for the kitchen and I followed her.

"Mom. Please don't add to the misuse of that phrase."

"What?" She started unloading the dishwasher.

"Mom, will you look at me?"

She turned and faced me.

"It's time we started expressing how we really feel more. I know I upset you this morning."

She let out a strangled cry and then pushed the back of her wrist to her mouth.

"You're a mom, not an android. I know you have

feelings. You're allowed to show them sometimes. I won't think any less of you. In fact, I think that will help me get to know you better."

She pulled me into a hug.

"We're not perfect and we shouldn't have to be." I reached up and ran my hand over her hair, messing it up.

"Gia." She smoothed it back down.

I laughed. I knew she wouldn't change in that instant or even overnight but this felt like a start.

CHAPTER 39

• • • • • • •

I closed my eyes, visualizing what I would say when I went on the stage in front of the whole school for the rally. My main focus was getting the seniors excited about graduation and especially the sober grad party I'd spent the last couple of months organizing. What had started off as another bullet point for my resume had ended up being something I was looking forward to. Especially after Marcus had told me his band would play.

It was loud out there, the entire student body smashed into the gym. From where I stood behind the thick curtain, the sound pressed into me. I took three deep breaths, my speech perfected, my confidence up. Daniel stood next to me, ready to take the stage with me even though he rarely spoke to the group. Hearing our names called over the speakers, we stepped out from behind the curtain. I could sense a slight change in the reaction of the audience to me. Normally there were loud cheers and whistles. Today along with those there was also a lower murmur. Not from everyone but from some. It was the first time I realized that my actions had a broader effect than just within my circle of friends.

I took the mic and cleared my throat. "Hello, everyone! Welcome to the last rally of the year! Who's ready for summer?" Beside me, Daniel raised his hands in the air and gave a loud shout.

There was a collective roar from the audience but it too was followed by some more murmuring. It threw me off. My speech that I had practiced seconds ago was slipping away. My eyes shot around the gym and landed on Claire. Hers was the safe face I had always searched for in the crowd on the few times I'd lost my composure. It wasn't a safe face today and only made the rest of my speech leave my brain.

"I'm sorry," I heard my voice echo through the gym. Daniel let out a surprise grunt from beside me. I hadn't meant to say it out loud but I had so I kept going. "I made a mistake. No, I won't be vague like that. I'll own up to it. I lied. I've been lying to my friends for the past month or so. Over something I didn't need to. Mainly because I didn't trust that my friends would still be my friends if I told the truth. And also because I was very self-absorbed and wasn't thinking beyond my own problems. What's wrong with me?"

It was a rhetorical question but someone from the audience yelled, "Nothing. You're still hot." Laughter bounced off the walls with that comment.

I rolled my eyes. "Yeah, thanks. That didn't really help. My point is I messed up. And Claire, Laney, Jules, I'm sorry. And actually, anyone else who heard about it and was disappointed in me, I'm sorry to you too. I'm trying to be better. I want to be better."

During my speech I had looked around, took in the room, delivered a message, but now my eyes sought out Claire again. I bit the inside of my cheek when I saw the cold look still on her face.

"I'm sorry." I handed the microphone to Daniel. "Save this rally," I whispered. "Get them excited for sober grad."

"I can't. I don't know what to say." His expression registered panic.

"Just be fun. You always are."

The panic left his face with that comment. "I am, aren't I?"

I smiled, squeezed his arm, and left to the sounds of Daniel chanting, "Sober grad" over and over.

Marcus and his band were good, really good, and I wasn't the only one who thought so. Most of the students that had come to sober grad night were dancing and attempting to sing along with the songs they'd never heard before. And considering none of them was drunk—the whole point of sober grad night—that had to mean the band was bringing them to this state of entertained. I gave Marcus a thumbs-up when he met my eyes. He seemed to laugh a little, like that wasn't the correct way to express my approval. There was some sort of "rock on" sign but I had no idea what it was. That was probably what I was supposed to use.

I scanned the crowd again. Things felt different tonight. Normally people were saying hi or talking to me, trying to catch my eye. Tonight eyes drifted past mine without thought or interest. Things had shifted. It didn't sting as much as I thought it would. I didn't deserve to be noticed any more than anyone else, especially because I rarely tried to notice people back. I was still working on being better about that.

There *was* a group that was getting a lot of notice. I hadn't thought Claire, Laney, and Jules would come, not after their reaction to my public apology. Dirty looks during the rally had been followed by complete radio silence since, but they had come. It wasn't to make up with me, though, because they'd pointedly ignored me all night. And they were surrounded by people.

My boyfriend had his own graduation party tonight, and his sister, my only friend at the present time, was only a junior. So that's how I came to be all alone at an event I'd spent the last few months of my senior year organizing. But I was okay with that.

I'd graduated after thirteen years in public school. I'd probably be remembered, but I hoped I'd spend the next thirteen years of my life on something I could be remembered *for*.

"Hey, Gia." A deep voice called me out of my thoughts.

I smiled. "Blake, the ice cream man. Happy graduation."

"You too. This is a great party."

"Thanks. I had a lot of help."

The music stopped playing and Marcus said into the microphone, "The band is going to take a five-minute break. We'll play some prerecorded music."

Soon Marcus had set aside his guitar and was heading our way. I thought he was going to ask me about food or something but he just stopped in front of me and nodded. "Good crowd."

"Thanks for playing. They love you."

"Sure."

"Marcus, this is Blake."

The guys nodded at each other.

"Your band is really good," Blake said.

"Thanks. Despite being told otherwise recently, I think we're halfway decent." He winked at me. "Speaking of, where are your lovely friends tonight?"

"Um." I pointed to where Claire, Laney, and Jules were now dancing with a group of guys.

"You outgrew them?"

"I think they outgrew me."

"I disagree."

I don't know why those words made my eyes sting.

Someone grabbed me from behind and I let out a small yelp. Bec came into my view, so I could only assume the arms still wrapped around me belonged to Hayden. I tipped my head back to see him.

"You chose only the most laid-back teacher to serve as the security guard at the entrance," Bec said. She put her arm around Marcus, who gave her a side hug back.

I laughed. "You guys broke into the party?"

"'Broke in' is such strong wording. 'Let in' is a better way to put it."

"We thought you might be lonely," Hayden said in my ear, "but it looks like you're fine."

Marcus backed up while saying, "Looks like the boys

are ready to play again. See you." He paused about five steps away. "And, Gia, I was serious."

"Thanks." Should I be thanking someone about telling me I outgrew my friends? I looked over at Jules, who was whispering something in Claire's ear while pointing at someone else. Yes, maybe I was okay with moving on from them for now. Maybe this summer or next year Claire and I could patch things up. Claire caught my eye then before I could look away, and I thought her expression said there was hope. She gave me a small smile but then let Jules lead her toward the food table.

The band started playing again and Bec grabbed Blake's arm. "I have no idea who you are but let's dance. I have someone I need to make jealous." He shrugged and followed her. It was hard to tell if, sitting behind the drums, Nate had noticed Bec.

I turned to face Hayden.

"Should *I* be jealous?" he asked.

"Of what?" At first I thought he was talking about Bec but then I realized he meant Marcus. "Oh. Of course not." I cleared my throat and attempted my best low, husky voice. "I want to dance with you."

He raised his eyebrows. "Was that an imitation of a robot? No, wait. A robot who smokes."

I hit his chest. He gave me his smoldering stare and I was so happy that I didn't have to control my reaction this time. I grabbed a fistful of his shirt and pulled him toward me. Our lips collided.

"You don't have to be a statue, Gia. She's not painting a portrait," Bec said.

"Oh, right." I adjusted my position on the stool where I sat while her mom painted.

Hayden came into the room and stood peering over his mom's shoulder. "Are you really painting bones?"

"Bec gave me a good idea."

"I told you she didn't need you here," Bec said.

"Of course I need her here. She's my muse."

"I actually need to steal her," Hayden said.

"No, I'm in the zone."

"Just for a second. Bec, take over."

"I love how you all think anyone works as my muse," Olivia said in a huff.

Hayden took my hand and pulled me out of the room. Out in the dim hall he pressed me against the wall and kissed me.

"You stole me for that?" I asked with a laugh.

"Yes . . . I mean no. I stole you to tell you our plan is in motion. Nate is on his way over. You distracted her long enough for me to steal her phone and text him."

I smiled. "Nice. Payback is so fun."

"And immature."

"So immature. Is she going to kill us?"

"Absolutely. But in the meantime . . ." His lips found mine again and I relaxed into him.

ACKNOWLEDGMENTS

● ● ● ● ● ● ●

As I sit down to write my fifth set of acknowledgments, I am still just as thankful as I was with the first set I wrote. I know that not everybody gets to do what they love, and I will be forever grateful to the people who make this possible for me. First, my readers. I can say that now. I actually have readers. And some of them actually seem to like me. You have no idea how happy this makes me. Because of you, I get to continue writing, and I am so grateful for that.

A big thank-you to my husband, Jared, who makes it much easier for me to write. He's the best support a girl could have. Plus, after seventeen years of marriage, I still like the guy. I mean, I always love him, but I like him too. My kids are quite awesome as well. I'm going to start with the youngest first, this time, since he always has to go last: Donavan, Abby, Autumn, and Hannah. They make me laugh every day and I've never been more proud of anyone in my life than I am of them.

My agent, Michelle Wolfson, has made being in this sometimes-difficult industry a lot easier for me. Without her, I'd be a mess. Thanks for everything, Michelle. I've also had the privilege to work with a couple of different editors for this book, both of whom were great—Sarah Landis and Catherine Wallace. Thanks for loving my books, ladies, and helping to make them better. And thanks to HarperTeen for giving me such an amazing push into the world of young adult literature. It's a great place to be. A special mention to some other members of my HarperTeen team: Stephanie Hoover, Rosanne Romanello, and Jennifer Klonsky.

Before I even let my agent or editor see my books, these lovely ladies have to suffer through the early drafts. They are some of my favorite people ever: Candice Kennington, Stephanie Ryan, Jenn Johansson, Renee Collins, Natalie Whipple, Sara Raasch, Michelle Argyle, Melanie Jacobson, Kari Olson . . . oh no, I'm forgetting someone, I just know it. I'm sorry if I forgot you.

Sometimes I don't write; I actually do other things (I know, I'm shocked too). These people try to remind me that it shouldn't be all books, all the time: Elizabeth Minnick, Rachel Whiting, Claudia Wadsworth, Brittney Swift, Mandy Hillman, Emily Freeman, Jamie Lawrence, Melanie Martinez, Amy Burbidge, and Erynn Nelson.

Last and least (just kidding, never least) is my amazing family. I've been blessed with a big one, and I know I am who I am today because of them: of course, my mom and dad (Chris and Don), Heather Garza, Jared DeWoody, Spencer DeWoody, Stephanie Ryan, Dave Garza, Rachel DeWoody, Zita DeWoody, Kevin Ryan, Vance and Karen West, Eric and Michelle West, Sharlynn West, Rachel and Brian Braithwaite, Angie and Jim Stettler, Emily and Rick Hill, and all their respective children.

Phew. When I finish, I always feel like I named everyone and their mother and at the same time forgot everyone and their mother. How is this possible? I'm so sorry if I forgot you. Please know it's because I have mush brain, not because you're not important.

Stephanie Ryan Photography

KASIE WEST lives with her family in central California, where the heat tries to kill her with its 115-degree stretches. She graduated from Fresno State University with a BA degree that has nothing to do with writing. Visit her online at www.kasiewest.com.